THE
BOOK
EXCHANGE

THE LAW-BRINGERS

The Law-Bringers

ELLIOT CONWAY

A Black Horse Western

ROBERT HALE · LONDON

Photoset in North Wales by
Derek Doyle & Associates, Mold, Clwyd.
Printed and bound in Great Britain by
WBC Book Manufacturers Limited,
Bridgend, Mid-Glamorgan.

For my great-nephew,
Adrian Hill

ONE

Only full-blooded hate and the bittersweet thought of vengeance, a life for a life, kept Billy Joe in the saddle and his grip on his sanity. Billy Joe was a slight-framed youth, too young, a man would have opined, to be carrying so much hate inside him. But, having buried his shot-down pa and butchered ma and his two kid sisters, escaping death himself by a hair's breadth, a coming-up-to eighteen-years-old Billy Joe had amassed more hate in a single day than several men would acquire in a lifetime.

The day on the ranch had begun as normally as any other day. He and his pa riding out to check on the sixty or so longhorns his pa ran, ma and the girls tending to the growing patch and the ranch livestock. As they reached the draw where the cattle were bedded down he and his pa were suddenly fired on by men on the valley rim. Billy Joe heard his pa cry out and saw him fall out of his saddle, then a red-hot iron was forcibly laid across his right temple, knocking him off Jubla,

7

his mule, in one blinding flash of pain, into the deep, black pit of unconsciousness.

Billy Joe came to at the bottom of the brush-choked dry wash that snaked across the front of the draw. He climbed out of it with a pounding head and as sick inside as a man seeking the hair of the dog after a heavy session in some bar. He felt the uncomfortable tightness of the skin on the right side of his face and, putting up a hand, touched a thin mask of dried blood. Reaching higher he gingerly fingered the bullet furrow along his brow, an action that increased the sickening pain he was suffering, almost causing him to black out again. Billy Joe reckoned he had been damn lucky not to have been killed. His pa's luck had run out. He found him lying in an unmoving, crumpled heap, his body shot through and through, many of the shells shot into him after he had already been killed. And Billy Joe knew then just how lucky he had been by falling into the wash out of sight of the raiders. This was the moment in time when Billy Joe's hate began to flame.

The cattle had gone, so had his pa's bay but, thankfully, Jubla came trotting out of the brush to greet him. Swimming-headed he hoisted his pa's body on to the saddle and scrambled up to perch by the seat of his pants on Jubla's ass. With one hand holding his pa in place, the other tight-gripping the reins, he dug his heels into Jubla's ribs and raced back to the ranch at a limb-risking pace. He had no idea how long he had lain at the bottom of the wash but the tight knot of sickness chewing away in the pit of his stomach like something alive told him that he would be too late to stop the raiders from carrying out what they intended doing at the ranch.

On seeing the column of smoke rising above the trees as he closed on the ranch Billy Joe realized, with terrible finality, that his worst fears were about to be confirmed.

Billy Joe's ma and two sisters lay like broken rag dolls in front of the smouldering backdrop of the burnt-out house. With limbs outstretched, clothes ripped and flung back, naked from the waist down, they had been brutally used then killed by savage, flesh-mutilating knife thrusts. Billy Joe howled like a mad dog in his sorrow. The anger and the hate against the men who had destroyed his family became almost too much for him to bear.

Billy Joe was ill-prepared to ride out on his vengeance trail. There was several days feed for Jubla but what food and dry rations there had been in the cabin had been destroyed by the fire. His handgun was a long-barrelled, cap and ball, Whitneyville Walker .44 Colt. His rifle, though just as ancient, was a long-firing, sixteen-load Henry. Both guns had been hidden by his pa in the furthermost barn from the shack as insurance against any Indian raid cutting him off from the guns in the cabin.

Billy Joe's thirst for blood didn't allow him to think too long and deep that his vengeance trail could turn out to be his suicide trail. For the number of men he was setting off to track down, a field-piece and a Gatling gun would not have come amiss, if Jubla could have been persuaded to haul them along. With one last lingering look at the four freshly dug earth mounds, Billy Joe, face all bony angles, devoid of all emotions, pointed Jubla's nose south-west, in the direction his pa's cattle had been driven.

Billy Joe had established that there were at least seven/eight raiders, riding iron-shod horses so it hadn't been a bronco-Indian, liquor-inspired killing raid. They could have been hard-asses, down from the Panhandle, or from the badlands of New Mexico; men who would willingly kill to get their hands on some cattle without parting with any cash. Billy Joe didn't think so, reckoning that even the stomping men of west Texas would draw the line at raping and killing three women. Another pointer against the raiders being Texans was the fact that the cattle were being driven due south, south to the Rio Grande and old Mexico. Billy Joe's face grew even leaner. It seemed to be on the cards that he was hunting down the Mexican bandit chief, with the fancy handle of Don Jose Valiente.

That surprised him. He knew of the Don's cattle and horse-lifting forays across the Rio Grande but the *bandido* chief hadn't raided this far north of

the border before. He would have to step carefully.
It wouldn't be easy to get close enough to the
murdering son-of-a-bitch to be able to draw a bead
on him with the Henry. But he owed it to his dead
family to try.

Six miles along the trail, Billy Joe saw that his
pa's herd had been joined by more cattle, several
hundreds of them and, adding to his considerable
worries, the number of raiders had swelled to over
thirty riders. Billy Joe's heart sank. In no way
could he take on a small army, unless he had the
cannon and the Gatling, and someone to fire
them. Cold logic tempered his mad haste for
revenge. It was a waste of time to even think of a
plan by which he could get face to face with the
Don. All he could do was to trail the raiders back
to their hideout in Mexico and trust to Lady Luck,
or whatever, to give him a few seconds'
opportunity to pump several .44 Henry shells into
the Don's stinking hide. What happened to him
after that would depend on the same kind of luck
holding out. Though to be truthful Billy Joe hadn't
planned his life that far ahead.

Don Jose Valiente, riding slightly ahead of the
stolen herd, thin-lipped smiled, though it brought
little warmth to the cold-eyed, high-cheek-boned
face, as he saw the sheen of water, the Rio Brava,
in the distance. Soon the herd and his men would
be in Chihuahua, out of reach of any *gringo*
retaliation against his latest raid on their

territory. Another battle against the hated
Yankees won.

Don Jose was not just a fancy handle as Billy
Joe had opined; pure Spanish blood flowed
through the Don's veins. The first Valiente in the
then called, New Spain, had waded ashore with
Cortez and the rest of the *conquistadors,* the
family line growing, prospering over the cen-
turies. Being what the *gringos* called stomping
men the Valientes became rich and powerful
hidalgos, the walls of their *hacienda* enclosing
hundreds of square miles, built by the sweat and
tears of the thousands of peons and Indian slaves,
held by the shedding of the blood of Mexicans,
Indians and, in the later years, the North
American *gringos*, who craved for a piece of the
Valientes' vast holdings.

Unfortunately for Don Jose his family *hacienda*
had been on land north of the Rio Brava in the
Mexican territory of Texas. The ever increasing
numbers of Yankee settlers moving south into
Texas became a threat to the Spanish-Mexican
landowners. Don Jose found the newcomers
arrogant, boastful, land-hungry men calling the
Latins greasers, treating them no better than the
Indian *pacificos,* taking what they wanted by the
pistol and the blade, as Don Jose's ancestors had
done.

The Yankee threat developed into a full-blown
war in 1847. Don Jose fought in that war being
wounded in the battle of the *Buena Vista*

Hacienda. The outcome of the war was that the *gringos* took all the Mexican territory north of the river the *gringos* decided to rename the Rio Grande, now the border between the United States and the republic of Mexico, leaving Don Jose almost penniless, unable to keep up the high living, the women, wine and gambling, a regular officer in a crack cavalry regiment was expected to follow.

The lifestyle of a poor *hidalgo* didn't appeal to Don Jose. He was determined to get back into the high society of the Spanish blue-bloods. That needed great wealth, a commodity he was short of. And he hadn't the time, or the inclination, to start building up the Valiente fortunes again. He would be too old to enjoy the pleasures he was missing out on. The time-honoured way for a man to get his hands on sizeable amounts of money fast was by stealing it from someone who had plenty. The men whom he would take it from, Don Jose decided, were the hated *gringos* who had stolen it from him in the first place. To satisfy his honour he told himself that he wasn't acting like a *bandido* but a soldier carrying on fighting the war of '47.

The new soldiers the Don commanded may have been barefooted, ragged-assed, grandmother-throat-cutters but he ruled over them with the iron hand of unbending discipline, shooting dead in an instant any of his men who dared to even raise a quizzical eyebrow at a given command.

The raping and the killing of the three *gringo* woman didn't go against Don Jose's way of thinking that he was conducting a military campaign against the Yankees. He was only allowing his men the privileges and pleasures that victorious soldiers throughout the ages had enjoyed.

Don Jose pulled his horse round to ride back along the left flank of the herd, slowing up beside Isidro Amayo, his sergeant, a hatchet-faced breed.

'Pull back with eight men, Sergeant,' he ordered. 'And take up positions on that ridge we've crossed. Just in case the *gringo* Ranger pigs try to stop us.'

'Si, Capitan,' Sergeant Amayo replied, touching his hat in a resemblance of a military salute.

Billy Joe calculated that he had been riding across Mexican territory for something like three hours when he noticed that a small bunch of the cattle he was tracking had been cut out of the herd and been driven west towards a distant line of hills. He judged that the Don was beginning to split up the herd for easier grazing needs. Since crossing the Rio Grande he had travelled over hell's own landscape with hardly enough grass growing to feed a herd of goats let alone a big bunch of hungry longhorns.

Billy Joe rode ahead a piece, pulling up his mule on a slight rise that gave him a good sighting along the trail the main herd had continued on.

He could see no sign of the cattle, the men driving them, or the lingering dust clouds their passage would have raised. He gave a grunt of satisfaction. There was a strong possibility, he thought, that an opportunity had come his way to strike the first blow of revenge against the destroyers of his family. He rode back to where the herd had split up and, leaning low across his saddle, he rode slowly along the new trail, examining the tracks more closely. By his reckoning there were only four riders with the cows and, what quickened his blood, he had seen one of the horse's tracks in the dust outside his house. A horse that had a peculiar back leg, kicking-out gait.

With a grim resolute smile Billy Joe then straightened up in his saddle and knee'd his mount into a ground-eating canter. M'be the other three men had taken part in the raping and killing of his ma and sisters. If they had then his revenge would really be sweet. If they hadn't it made no matter. He had every intention of killing all the sons-of-bitches. A metering out of summary justice for cattle-lifters any Texas court would uphold.

Billy Joe rode through a sparse stand of alomas, then guided Jubla over a shallow, loose-stoned arroyo whose water he reckoned must be responsible for the grass and trees in this corner of the badlands. Beyond the wash Billy Joe heard the bellowing of cows he could not yet see. He quickly dismounted, drawing out the Henry as he

swung to the ground. He checked the actions and
loads of both the Henry and the Walker and,
leaving his horse tied to a stone at the wash, he
went forward on foot, the Henry held high across
his chest ready for instant snap-shot firing.

The cattle were grazing in a gently sloping-
sided basin and Billy Joe, lying prone on its rim,
looked down at the opposition with nerves so
screwed-up he had difficulty in breathing. He had
been right in his first reading of the tracks, there
were four of the raiders. All he had to do now was
to see them well and truly dead without him
becoming likewise.

The moment of truth had arrived for Billy Joe.
He was realizing that solemn grave-side
promises, however powerfully and honestly given,
had to come to terms with life or death,
cold-blooded reality. There were four men down
there, *pistoleros,* brutal murderers and, although
he was a fine shot with the Henry, he had never
drawn a bead on a man before let alone killed one,
though he felt that his conscience would not stop
him from pulling the trigger of the Henry. After
all he was only shooting down wild dogs.

That still didn't help any in lowering the odds
he was going to face. Billy Joe slow-smiled. He
wasn't on his own. He had a bunch of *gringo*
longhorns to back him up. A fire under their tails
could cause such a helluva ruckus that would
distract the raiders more than somewhat, giving
him time to cut down m'be two of them before they

cottoned on to the fact that they were under attack.

Billy Joe sidled back from the edge of the basin then drew out his knife and began to force the shell cases off a handful of the Henry's reloads. When he opined that he had enough of the grey powder for what he had in mind he got to his feet and ran to the far side of the hollow. Here he found that the grass was long and yellow, easier to set on fire. And the herd was between him and the four raiders squatting at a campfire. More important, the wind was blowing from behind him, across the basin. With a bit of luck, Billy Joe thought, the longhorns might put paid to the sons-of-bitches for him.

Billy Joe sprinkled the gunpowder at the base of a thick tuft of grass and put a lighted match to it and stepped back. The powder sizzled and flared into flames, fanned by the wind into a rapidly spreading, waist-high wall of fire. The herd gave one mass bellow of fright and spooked, taking off with a noise like rolling thunder.

The flames died away as they reached the flattened, fouled grass where the herd had been and Billy Joe walked slowly down into the dip, hawk-eyeing the still lingering smoke and dust haze, the Henry held halfway to his shoulder. A raider, coughing and rubbing at his eyes stumbled into view. Billy Joe saw the Mexican's face twist in angry alarm as his hand clawed for the pistol sheathed on his right hip. Billy Joe stopped in his stride and, in one fluid movement, brought the Henry up into his shoulder, aimed and fired. The two shots tore into the raider's throat, the blood coming away from his neck in a fast, life-ending red fountain as the powerful impact of the .44 shells lifted him off his feet and flung him to the ground.

A pistol cracked, causing Billy Joe to spin round. Limping towards him from the other edge of the dip came a second bandit, firing wildly at him from the hip. He heard the ominous hiss of a shell passing too close for comfort as he squeezed off a single load at this new threat. With a squeal like a wounded horse the raider keeled over, both of his legs busted.

The smoke and dust clouds had lifted and Billy Joe couldn't see any signs of the two remaining raiders making their play. He tugged out the Walker from his pants top and thumbing back the hammer he walked across to the writhing, loudly groaning raider.

Face working in agony, clutching at his blood-soaked left thigh, the raider spat what Billy Joe reckoned was a string of Spanish cuss words, at him.

'You ain't no more than a mite winged,' he said. 'I could have easily put a shell through your dirty, mean-faced head but I've something special for you in mind, a small payment for what you and the scum you ride with did in Texas. I don't know if you can savvy *gringo* talk but if you can I'd advise you to say your prayers, if you know how to, because I intend stringing you up on one of those trees back along the trail there. That should pass the message along to your boss, that no-good, murderin' asshole, the Don, that he ain't about to ride into Texas free and easy any more.'

Billy Joe had more curses mouthed at him and he noticed what little colour there was in the raider's pain-creased face had drained away. He gave a savage grin. 'I reckon you've got the gist of what I've said.' He bent down and picked up the wounded man's dropped pistol and stuffed it in his shirt. 'I don't want you to think that you could m'be down me when my back's turned, or end your misery by putting a bullet in your head and deny me the pleasure of stringing you up. You just lie there and, as I said, try prayin', while I go and see what's happened to the two no-good murderers who ride with you. If they're still breathing I could soon be having a real ball.'

The air had cleared completely in the basin and Billy Joe picked out two grotesque, twisted-limbed figures lying motionless at the foot of the rim he had first looked down on the cattle. His luck had surely been riding high. He would never again call a longhorn a brainless, ornery, flea-ridden critter.

Slowly his nerves began to unwind. He gently eased the hammer of the Colt forward and slipped it into the waistband of his pants and walked to the still cursing raider, and a hanging.

Billy Joe caught up with the herd more or less still bunched up. The raiders' horses hadn't suffered the same fate as two of their owners had and, on seeing him and Jubla, stopped trailing the cattle and closed in on him. The herd had slowed down to a shuffling walk in the direction of the nearest water, the Rio Grande.

Billy Joe's opening shots in his war against the Don had dictated his next moves in the campaign. Soon the Don would discover his losses in the basin then turn over every rock in Chihuahua to find out who was responsible. For him to stay in Chihuahua, a land he didn't know, and in which he had no friends, was foolhardily dangerous. When his rations ran out it would be even too risky to go into a village to buy fresh supplies in case word was passed on to the Don that a *gringo* stranger was in the territory. The Don would put two and two together and, coming up with the right answer, the big hunt would be targeted on him. And he would be as good as dead.

The best tactics he could adopt, Billy Joe thought, was to cross back into Texas, sell the spare horses to buy supplies and keep up a lone vigil along the stretch of the Rio Grande he had forded coming into Mexico, hoping that the Don would come out raiding again then play it from there. With the same sort of luck he added hopefully.

He also decided, if he could, that he might as well rub the Don's nose well and truly in the shit by driving the cattle across the border. The Texas Rangers would see to it that they were returned to their rightful owners. Billy Joe looked over his shoulder for any signs of riders ass-kicking up his back-trail. Seeing no fast, closing-in dust clouds he pulled out his pistol and, riding round the drag, fired off all its loads in the air. The noise set the cattle heading north for the Rio Grande in a lumbering, ground-trembling run.

TWO

Texas Ranger Sergeant Buckley Taylor pulled up his mount at the edge of the slow-flowing stretch of the Rio Grande and rested back in his saddle, bushed and frustrated. The tracks of the stolen cattle his four-man patrol had been trailing ended on the strip of sand that led to the wet-back crossing. Buck, middle-aged, stockily built, face plainsman-weathered, cursed long and loud, then screwed round in his saddle to look at his men with dust-reddened eyes.

'Boys,' he said, 'the sonuvabitch has beaten us again. We'll have to prevail on the Capt'n to take the whole company across this river and flush out that sidewinder, Don Jose Valiente, from his hole-up and to hell with the stink the Mex Government will raise against us *gringos* for invadin' their territory. Him and his cutthroats are runnin' us Rangers ragged trying to catch up with them before they slip back across the Rio Grande after barin' their asses at us.'

State law was coming to post-war Texas but

still too slow to ease the pressure on the only
law-enforcers in some parts of the State, the
Rangers. Buck got to wondering just how Stephen
Austin's original ten Rangers upheld the law in
the land they rode over. In '23 Austin, the first big
Yankee rancher in the then Mexican-ruled Texas,
hired ten men to range over his land protecting
his stock. They were to uphold *gringo* Texas law;
they were the first Texas Rangers. Those days the
Comanche and the Apache were raising a fire and
blood hell across the land. Now, thank God, Buck
thought, only a few *broncos*, the last of the red
hold-outs, were living in the old style, raiding and
killing white eyes. Buck's face stoned over. But
that bloodthirsty Mex son-of-a-bitch, the Don, and
his small army of *bandidos* had taken over from
the Apache and Comanche marauding warbands.
Riding out of their hole-up in the Candelaria
mountains across the river in Mexico, able to cross
the Rio Grande unseen at a score of places, their
regular excursions on to American soil made
ranchers and farmers in the border regions too
scared to sleep in their beds at night, stretching
the thin line of law-bringers to their limit, keeping
men like him and his patrol hard-assing it along
the Rio Grande chasing elusive, death-dealing
shadows.

Buck spat disconsolately between his horse's
ears then swung himself out of his saddle. 'We'll
bed down here for the night,' he growled. 'The
horses need a rest as much as us. We'll head back

to El Paso in the morning and report in. I reckon that the Don won't be poking his dirty snout across the Rio Grande for a spell. By the readin' of these tracks he's got what he came to Texas for. I'll put it to the Capt'n that it will take the whole company, and a regiment of soldier boys to keep the Don penned in on his own side of the border. Or go across the border ourselves and beard the bastard in his den, if we knew exactly where it was.'

The horses had been fed and watered, the campfire lit, and coffee coming to the boil when Ranger Cassidy standing the first watch at the river's edge raised the sudden alarm.

'A big bunch of riders comin' up to the crossin', Sarge!' he yelled.

Cursing, the Rangers leapt to their feet, grabbing for their rifles, one of them kicking the coffee pot over, and ran down to the river, Buck leading the mad scramble.

Cassidy favoured his sergeant with a pinched-assed look. 'If it's the Don, Sarge,' he said, 'he's brought enough *hombres* with him to fight the battle of the Alamo all over again. Four rifles won't stop them any.'

An equally worried-faced Buck, keeping his disturbing thoughts to himself, brought up his army glasses and gave the dust cloud moving on the river at a fair pace a long searching look. Slowly his expression changed. Grinning widely he lowered the glasses and turned to Cassidy.

'You can stop feeling that you have an urgent need to pay a visit to the crapper, Cass. It ain't a bunch of greaser *bandidos* comin' our way. The dust is bein' raised by a herd of honest to goodness Texas beef.' Buck focused the glasses once more on to the dust cloud. Still keeping the glasses up to his eyes he said, 'As far as I can make out there's only one man drivin' the longhorns though I can make out another four saddle-horses. It ain't likely that he's a one man band of cattle-lifters. I reckon the fella's all that's left of a cattle outfit after meeting up with big trouble further south, Don trouble m'be, and is endeavourin' to get the herd back to Texas.' Buck put the glasses back into their case and gave out his orders.

'Pat, get back to the camp and make the coffee. I opine that *hombre* nursin' the cattle will appreciate a pail full of it when he gets this side of the river. The rest of us will wait here and give him a hand to bring the cattle over. But keep a close eye on him just in case I've figured him wrong.'

Billy Joe spotted the men waiting on the Texas side of the crossing and, giving Jubla a heel in the ribs, wheeled clear of the herd and its trail dust and raised the Henry horizontally above his head, a gesture of peace. He didn't doubt that the men were Texicans and would not harbour any ill will towards him, if they knew who he was. From where they were standing he could be a Mex *bandido,* a *gringo owlhooter* even, pushing along a

herd he had no bill of sale for. And since the Don
had started his raiding on American soil the golden
rule along the border was to shoot first at any
suspicious characters and do the talking when the
gunsmoke had settled.

As the first of the cattle plunged into the water,
Buck ordered his three Rangers to keep the cattle
in line then he swam his horse across the Rio
Grande to help to bring up the drag. He was also
keen to find out how it came about that only one
man was in charge of the herd, and the significance
of the four riderless horses. Buck wasn't surprised
to note that it was only a youth, eighteen or
nineteen years old, driving the cattle. A kid had to
take on man's chores before he put a razor to his
face in the frontier regions. What did set him
wondering was the dead-eyed look the kid gave
him when he drew up his horse alongside him. It
was a look that grew on a man living under great
pressure or danger for a long time. A battle-weary
soldier's or a wild, trail-end town marshal's look.
The kid must have got his overnight.

'Sergeant Buckley, Texas Rangers,' Buck said.
And left his introduction at that. It wasn't the time
and definitely not the place to enquire into a man's
business. 'You don't mind me and my men giving
you a hand to get your cattle across. This is *mal
hombres* territory, Don Jose Valiente and his wild
boys' stompin' ground. It don't do to linger this side
of the Rio Grande. I take it that you've heard of the
son-of-a-bitch?'

Billy Joe smiled and Buck got the unnerving impression that an Apache, just before he lifted some unfortunate asshole's hair, would give a likewise cold, cock-a-hoop grin. Billy Joe nodded in the direction of the four horses.

'They belonged to four of his men. I shot one, strung up another and the longhorns here stomped the other two into the dirt. These are some of the cattle he lifted on his last raid. I kinda thought it right and proper to return them to their real owners.'

Again Buck saw the similarity between Billy Joe's face and a reservation-jumping buck's more so now that his smile had gone. 'Then I intend to try and put the Don on the fast train to hell where he belongs,' ended Billy Joe.

Buck had seen many blowhard kids in the saloons at El Paso and Austin trying to build up reps as genuine hard-nosed shootists. But the matter-of-fact way this fearful-eyed kid had told him that he was gunning for the most notorious killer, on both sides of the border, didn't sound like boastful talk to him. Suicidal, madman's talk m'be. Yet the kid didn't look *loco*, and he had seen off four of the Don's men on his own. Whatever state of mind the kid was in, one thing was for sure, a big hate was burning him up wanting to get himself dead so soon.

'I'm Billy Joe Foy, Mr Buckley,' Billy Joe said, and told the Ranger of the raid and the killing of all his family. 'So you see I've every reason to track the Don down and kill him. Blood calls for blood.' The cheerless smile broke out on Billy Joe's face once more. 'I got some blood back in repayment. At least one of the sonsuvbitches I killed took part in the raid on our farm.'

'You've sure got balls to go on your own into the Don's backyard, Mr Foy,' Buck said. 'Even though you've got a mighty good reason for doin' so.' But Buck was thinking that for whatever reason, up on a mule, armed only with a museum piece cap and ball pistol and an equally ancient Henry, it was an undertaking of a crazy-thinking kid. And one the kid would never get the luck to pull off again. 'I'd appreciate it if once we get the cattle across you'll stay a spell at our camp,' Buck continued. He grinned. 'I opine that you'll not turn down the offer to partake in some warm beans and fresh coffee. Then you can tell me if you've picked up any pointers to where the Don rests up between raids.' Buck's face hardened. 'One day we Rangers, a full company of us, will have to take a trip into Mexico and put the Don out of the raidin' business for keeps. But before my capt'n will contemplate such an irregular action he'll want to know just exactly where the Don is. We *gringos* can't go ass-kickin' it all over Chihuahua lookin' for him, because there's more than a fair chance we could end up exchangin' lead with a *rurale* patrol and start another Mex war.' Buck smiled again. 'That's enough small talk for now, let's get the rest of these beeves back on United States territory.'

* * *

Buck knew that Billy Joe Foy was *loco*, driven that way by the butchering of his family. When the kid told him of his intentions to prowl along the Rio Grande and jump on the Don and his *muchachos* if they showed up this side of the river it gave him a clearer insight into just how crazy he was.

Buck had moved camp, and the herd, into a secluded box canyon, five, six miles back from the Rio Grande, figuring that the Don would be as crazy as the kid was when he discovered four of his boys killed and the cattle gone. His pride having been hurt he would scout out the trail of the cattle, and the men who had done the deed. It wouldn't need an expert tracker to follow the cattle tracks to the Rio Grande. Seeing the cattle grazing on the other side of the river would be too big a temptation for the Don not to come across and steal the longhorns all over again, saving face somewhat. Of course, Buck reasoned, the Don could have already made up his mind to come fireballing into Texas, mad-assed enough to trail his herd all the way to the Red if needs be.

'Help yourself to another plate of beans, Mr Foy,' Buck said. 'By what you've told me and the boys it's been a while since you've eaten.'

Billy Joe voiced his thanks and held out his plate for Cass to give him another generous helping of beans, wolfishly spooning them down.

Suddenly his hands began to shake and he felt icy chills all over his body, making him feel as though he was having an attack of swamp fever. Billy Joe reckoned that it was more than just being hungry and deadbeat, it was the reaction to the killings back there in Mexico. Killing, however right it was, didn't settle easy on a man who had been raised on the charitable teachings of the Good Book. Billy Joe's lips thinned. He would have to get used to it, the killings had hardly got started.

Buck narrow-eyed Billy Joe, seeing and understanding all the emotions mirrored on his face. Somehow he had to persuade the kid that on his own the Don and his gang would stomp him into the ground in their passing and not notice it. And only by joining the Rangers would he get an even chance of settling up with the Don. Buck wasn't just wanting to give Billy Joe the best opportunity to fulfil his sworn oath, he wanted him for the personal selfish reason that the kid would make a first-class Ranger in the hunt to rid the regions of the scourge of the Don. A man who has the big hate for the fella he's about to go up against is more likely to stick it out to whatever end than someone doing it only for the pay.

Buck knew that it wouldn't be easy swinging the kid's mind to his way of thinking. Billy Joe now had the frozen-faced, tight-lipped look of a one-track-minded *hombre*. He had an idea though that could get Billy Joe to El Paso and once there m'be somehow, he didn't know how yet, he could

delay him still further from riding out on his lone
mission. By then, Buck thought, the kid could
have toned down some, reasoning more calmly
and logically. Knowing himself what he was
doing, a one-man crusade, was foolish and
dangerous.

'I would be obliged, Mr Foy, if you would give
me a hand in getting the beef to El Paso,' he said.
'Just in case the Don takes it in his head to come
chasin' after them. You'll be another welcome
gun, not that it will make any difference to the
outcome if we do have a brush with the
sonuvabitch, but we could take a few more of them
down with us. And El Paso is a good place to sell
your extra horses and get supplies. If you try to
sell them to one of the few sutlers between here
and El Paso you'll not get a fair price for them.
The cutthroat-pricing bastards are used to robbin'
the Injuns.'

'I'll help you to drive the herd to El Paso,' Billy
Joe said. 'I've brung them this far I might as well
take them the whole hog. Besides, I owe you for
letting me share your rations.' There was also
another reason for offering to stay with the
Rangers. The sergeant and his men were
hard-headed plainsmen, unexpected allies in his
fight. Men with killing experience, good men to
walk the line with. And the Don and his raiders
could, at any time, come splashing across the Rio
Grande and draw the line.

Buck grinned across the fire at him. 'Any *hombre* who gets rid of four of the Don's *muchachos* is entitled to a slap-up dinner in the best eating-place in El Paso. You just get your head down after you've had your fill, Billy Joe. Me and my men will stand the watches.'

Though first light's chilling mists still hung over the encampment the sweat rolled down Isidro Amayo's cheeks and neck as freely as it had done two hours ago, humping his woman. This time it was with apprehension, not passion. Don Jose Valiente wasn't a sociable man even when things were going right for him. Forced by circumstances to live in a one-roomed shack in a remote canyon instead of some grandly furnished officer's quarters in Mexico City, pretty, sweet-smelling *señoritas* always at hand for the asking, tends to sour a man's outlook on life. And, right now, he was the bringer of bad news.

The men he had sent out to relieve the guards at one of the dispersed bunches of cattle had returned with the alarming, and unbelievable, news that their four *compañeros* had been killed and the cattle gone. It could only have been *gringos'* work, Amayo thought angrily. No Mexican would dare to steal from the Don let alone kill four of his *muchachos*. What mattered now, for his wellbeing, was to take immediate

action to try and get the cattle back and the
gringos caught, to be pinned out on some anthill,
before he told the Don of his loss. Otherwise the
Don would be looking for a new sergeant.

'Ride as fast as you can for the Rio Bravo,' he
said. 'You might catch up with the *gringos* who
have taken the cattle. If there too many of them
just try and delay them till the *capitan* and I come
with more men.' Amayo waved his arms in a
gesture of dismissal. *'Fuera! Fuera!* Go, go,
muchachos!'

As the riders thundered out of the camp Amayo
hurriedly dressed, foregoing the delights of the
arm and leg-clinging warmth of an aroused
woman. Then, going outside, he proceeded to kick
awake as many of the men he thought sober
enough to stay in their saddles after a night's
drinking and humping celebrating a successful
raid. Only then did he feel confident enough to
face the Don.

Through the open window of the Don's shack
Amayo heard the ever-heightening moans of a
woman being pleasured and he stayed his hand
from rapping at the door. He himself would shoot
any unfeeling *hombre* who interrupted him at
such a highly emotional time. He waited, still
perspiring, till the Don's latest bed companion's
moans ended in a single high-pitched shriek, and
still he waited, knowing well the Don's bull-like
virility. He heard someone moving about inside
and finally felt that it was good as time as any to

bring the Don into the unpleasant picture.

'*Mi Capitan,*' he called, before the Don had opened the door, in his eagerness not to prolong his nervousness any longer. 'Four men guarding one of the herds have been killed and the *gringo* sonsuvbitches have taken the cattle.'

The Don stood in the doorway, skull-face flushed with the excitement of his woman's athletic lovemaking. Only his eyes registered how he was taking the news of the killings. Amayo mentally crossed himself and said a silent prayer to the Holy *Madre* that the Don was bare-assed naked. If he had been in uniform and wearing his pistol, the evil-eyed look the Don was giving him would have been quickly followed by several bullets, all painfuly lingering killing shots. To deflect some of the Don's anger he let him know that while he was enjoying bouncing his woman in his big bed he hadn't been doing likewise.

'I have sent men out to follow the tracks, *mi Capitan,*' he said. Swallowing hard, waiting for the verbal storm to break, he added, 'And six men are ready to ride out on your orders.' Then thought whatever he had said or had done there would be no pleasing an *hombre* with the soul of a *diablo.*

The Don may have been a devil, and right now an angry one, but he had the logical mind of a trained military officer. It was his fault that the cattle had been stolen. He ought to have calculated that the Texas *gringos*, stung by his

constant raiding on their soil, would try some
raiding of their own. The cattle should have been
better guarded. But that presented him with a
problem. He wasn't commanding regular, well-
disciplined troops, soldiers who would obey
without question any given order, knowing the
fearful consequences of facing a firing squad if
they didn't. He was dealing with murderers,
thieves, the scum of Chihuahua. On a raid they
accepted his iron-fisted discipline but back in
camp they wanted to be left to enjoy their
pleasures. The Don grimaced; the rotgut liquor,
the foul-breathed, greasy-fleshed, over-weight
women. If he attempted to ride roughshod over
them, some morning Sergeant Amayo would find
him still in bed with his throat cut. Amayo had
been most fortunate to find six sober men in the
camp. Or he had a very persuasive boot.

Almost benignly he said, 'Good, Sergeant. I'll be
ready to ride out in ten minutes.'

As a surprised and relieved Amayo walked
across to the corral to see to it that the Don's horse
was saddled-up he heard the Don's woman's
shrieks again, with not a note of pleasure ringing
in them. Amayo blessed his good fortune for the
second time. *El Diablo* still sat on the Don's
shoulder.

The Don sat back in his saddle on the Mexican
side of the Rio Bravo, mentally digesting what
information he had been given from the men who

had trailed the herd to the river and the two he had sent into Texas to check out the trail there. Only one *gringo* had been responsible for the killing of his men and driving away the cattle. Who was he, this lone *gringo*? A hired *pistolero*? A Texas lawman? Whoever he was he had proved that he was a deadly threat to him. His judgement as a soldier had been found wanting, this time. His fearful reputation had made him too complacent. He wouldn't underestimate his *gringo* enemies again.

Across the river his scouts had discovered a deserted camp, twelve hours old, used by six men. The six men were now driving the cattle. Again, thinking like a soldier, the Don knew when it was the right time to do battle, to win. He didn't think that time was now. With only seven men, most of them hardly sober, without proper reconnaissance, to go headlong across the river was too risky an operation. They could easily catch up with the slow-moving cattle but the odds were too even, and they could meet up with more Texans. And somehow the mysterious lone *gringo*, a lynching-man, unconsciously disturbed him. He was what the military manuals called the unknown factor in any campaign, and a commander neglecting to assess such a factor risked losing his battle. The *gringo* could be watching them right now, planning his next moves.

The Don's face boned over. One thing was for sure, a tightening up of the camp's defences was called for. He would place men at strategic points along the river to give him early warning of any *gringos* crossing into Mexico and heading in the general direcion of his camp. The sight of their hanged and shot *compadres* should mute any complaints from his men having to do extra duties. Amayo glimpsed the look on his captain's face. The *diablo* inside the Don was openingly showing itself.

The Don pulled his horse around and looked at Amayo, the devil's look still there. 'The next time we pay a visit to Texas, Sergeant, where we ride over we will leave the land like the *gringo* General Sherman left Georgia.' Raising his voice he yelled, 'Come *muchachos,* let's ride back to our women!'

Amayo, riding in the Don's wake, didn't know who the *gringo* Sherman was or in what state he had left this place Georgia, the Don spoke of. He would be satisfied if he could *deflora* some *gringo* virgins as he had done on the last raid.

THREE

Seth Bishop, repairing a broken hinge on his hay barn door, heard the angry gobbling of a wild turkey in the thick clump of brush some forty feet away from him. Then another answering call further to his left among the apple trees. Although the hot Texas sun had been up for two hours Seth's blood chilled over. Struggling hard to act normally he swung the door to and fro several times as if testing his workmanship. Then he picked up his bag of tools and walked just as casually across to the house and the Winchester leaning up against a porch post. The longest short walk he was feeling he had ever made in his life.

Stepping on to the porch he grabbed for the rifle and, practically in the same sweeping movement, pushed his wife, Lill, stepping out on to the porch, back into the house, back-heeling the door shut behind them.

Lill Bishop's angry protest at her rough-handling died in her throat as she saw her husband's strained, ashen-faced look. The first

39

word he spoke, 'Comanche', only confirmed her already known fears.

'At least two of the red devils, skulking out there beyond the barn,' continued Seth as he barred the door and pulled the heavy shutters over the window. 'You get the other rifle and go and close the back door and the rest of the windows.'

Lill didn't move, only staring with open-mouthed horror at her husband.

'Move woman!' Seth snapped, nervously angry. 'Or the red varmints will be strolling into your kitchen!'

'Mollie's still outside; she's feeding the hogs!' Lill Bishop's words came out as a frantic, terrified scream, sounding like a death knell in Seth's ears. His stomach heaved, sickening as he thought of the terrible things the Comanche would do to his daughter if they got their hands on her.

Yet, unlike his wife he didn't appeal to his Maker for help. Seth had seen too many burnt-out shacks, their butchered occupants, to know, for whatever reason, God paid little heed to the pleas of Texas homesteaders when in perilous life or death situations. Their salvation lay with the help of well-aimed Winchesters and Colts. He did, under his breath though, curse and swear profanely and as fervently as any religious praying-man.

'You do what I told you to do, Lill,' he said, trying to keep his voice calm and soothing, masking his gut-churning worries for the safety of his daughter. 'I'll go and bring her in.'

A small fusillade of shells thucked into the door as he opened it, driving him back into the room. He quickly slammed it shut again, and did some more cursing. The way things were shaping up for the Bishop family, God, whether he believed in His goodness or not, seemed to be the only one who could save his daughter's life. Unless, he thought desperately, Mollie did what he had told her to if faced with suchlike circumstances. If the girl kept her head there was still a chance that she would come through this trouble alive. He turned and gave his wife a pale shadow of a confident smile.

'Don't you worry none about Mollie, Lill,' he said. 'She knows what she has to do when Injun trouble comes. Now, you get that rifle and be prepared to use it with good effect or your daughter won't have a home to come back to.'

Rifle fire shattering the window behind him put Seth's worries about his daughter's wellbeing temporarily at the back of his mind. Right now his and Lill's life were the ones in immediate danger. He heard Lill's rifle open up which proved that she also had managed to suppress her fears about Mollie enough to defend her man and home. More ominously to Seth it proved that the Comanche had the house ringed. The battle was well and truly joined.

Seth poked his rifle through the shutter's firing

slot and fired a rapid half load in a spreading arc
into the brush from where he had heard the first
of the turkey calls. He saw the brush shake as
though being buffeted by a strong wind. Then, to
his grim satisfaction, a man came out into the
opening, swaying from side to side in a drunk's
tanglefooted stumbling walk, hardly clearing the
brush before falling down on his face, to lie in an
unmoving crumpled heap. Seth saw that he had
guessed wrong about who the raiders were. The
first blood to the Bishops was definitely not a
Comanche, not any breed of Indian at all. So he
reckoned that it could be a band of border scum or
comancheros. Whoever they were, his and his
family's fate if they fell into their hands alive
would be no less fearful and terminal than if the
raiders had been *bronco* Comanche.

Mollie Bishop heard the gunfire and, for a
moment, the implication of what it could mean for
her froze her thinking processes; then dropping
the feed pail she reached out for the Dragoon Colt
resting on a shelf, the big pistol her pa had
insisted she should carry whenever she left the
house, in spite of its weight bruising her thigh as
she walked with it tucked in the top of her levis.

'But Pa,' she had protested, 'I'll only be a stone's
throw distance from the house!'

Her pa, hard-eyeing, said, 'It could come about
one day to be the range of a Comanche arrow
flight.'

Mollie shivered. Now that dreaded day had

come. The gunfire increased, one shot sounding just outside the covered-in hogpen. The big pistol wavered unsteadily as she thumbed back the hammer then, wild-eyed with fear, she held the Colt in both stretched-out hands aiming at the open doorway. Her pa had also told her to make for the hay barn and hide herself among the bales of hay in the loft. On no account must she show herself, or fire the pistol whatever was happening at the house. And her pa made her promise that if she was pushed into a real tight corner and had to use the pistol, she had to save the last load of the six-chambered Colt for herself.

Though Mollie knew that it would be a quicker and less terrible ending than being taken alive to be used by the Comanche bucks, if that time came she didn't think she would have the nerve to put a shell in her own head. But, to keep her solemn promise to her pa, she would keep one shell unfired. Mollie gritted her teeth with the determination of a born plainswoman, controlling her fears, but by heck, she thought, the other five loads she would use to help her ma and pa to beat off the raiders. She couldn't get to the barn without being seen, even if she had intended to and she'd be damned, thinking most unlady-like, if she was going to hide like some yellow hound-dog knee-deep in hog shit.

Billy Joe, nursing the left side of the herd, saw the Ranger riding point come ass-kicking it back to the herd to pull up alongside Sergeant Taylor riding watch on the far side of the drive. After a few minutes talk the sergeant rode towards the rear of the herd and swung left across the drag to catch up with him.

'I've just been told that there's gunfire away to your right, Mr Foy,' Buck said. 'There's a homestead a piece in that direction, a Seth Bishop, with a wife and daughter. It could be a Comanche trick to draw us away from the herd so that they can lift a few cows, or they're out on a real killing raid. There's also the possibility that Seth is having trouble with some of the Don's murderin' assholes. I'm goin' to have a look-see with one of my men but I'll take you along instead if you want to ride with me. Though I oughta tell you that it strictly ain't no concern of yours being that you ain't a Ranger.'

Billy Joe's face hardened and, without any hesitation, he said, 'I'll go with you, Sergeant Taylor. It makes no matter who is doing the raidin', they're my kind having trouble and I sure wouldn't like Mrs Bishop and her daughter to have done to them what my ma and sisters suffered.'

Buck marked up another mental plus for Billy Joe Foy in his assessing of the kid as a possible Texas Ranger. The kid wasn't as soured up inside with his own personal loss not to be able to risk his neck in helping out some poor son-of-a-bitch in what could be real shooting trouble. Buck grinned. 'Let's go, Billy Joe, and mete out some Texas Ranger justice if needs be!'

The flickering of the sunlight streaming through the wide-spaced planking on one side of the pen caught Mollie's eye. Alarmed, she swung round and saw the crouching bulk of a man, back towards her, creeping along the outside of the wall. Tight-lipped, hardly daring to breathe, she aimed the pistol at him, keeping him covered as he moved. She thought that her immediate danger had passed when suddenly, as if sensing her presence in the pen, the raider turned and a bearded, cruel face glared at her through the gaps between the planks. The glare changed to a surprised-eyed leer, more frightening to Mollie, as the raider realized he was eye-balling a young girl.

Mollie's silent scream of fear rang in her ears as loud as the thunderous crack of the Colt in the enclosed space of the pen did. The outline of the face was instantly blotted out in a spout of blood and pieces of facial bone. Mollie's scream was for real this time as, once more, unrestricted rays of sunlight shone into the pen.

The hogs driven wild by the sound of the shot broke down their holding-in gate, knocking Mollie off her feet in their mad, kicking and squealing scramble to get into the open. Mollie picked herself up, the backs of her hands bleeding, cut by the hogs' sharp hooves, clothes all torn and muddied. She groped frantically for the pistol that had fallen into the hog-dirt-strewn straw at the rear of the pen.

She was still on her knees, gagging, as she reached into the slimy, foul-smelling mess when hands grabbed hold of her hair and dragged her, kicking and screaming as wildly as the hogs, out of the pen. Then she was yanked brutally to her feet and her captor pulled her tight to his barrel chest.

'Lookee here, boys,' she heard her captor shout, and smelt liquor-laden breath. 'This young bitch has just blowed Luke's face clear away!'

Through the mist of tear-filled eyes Mollie glimpsed a pock-marked, unshaven face, long greasy black hair, tied back Indian style. She was also conscious of a body heat and odour as nauseating as the hogpen smells.

'Missee,' the raider said, 'I know a certain Injun chief below the border who'll pay a rare price for you. That's if you ain't been used before.' He favoured her with a broken-toothed, blood-curdling grin. 'And I can keep the rest of the boys from havin' their pleasure with you.'

Molly tried to wriggle and claw her way out of his grasp but the cold edge of a knife pressing against her neck stiffened her rigid in terror.

'You there in the shack!' the raider yelled. 'I've got your girl! If you don't come out all peaceful-like for starters I'm goin' to begin carving lumps out of her face!'

Seth heard the threat but still held onto his rifle till his wife came out of the kitchen and put a hand on his shoulder. 'We'll have to go out, Seth,' she said softly but firmly. 'Mollie's life is more important than all this,' making a sweeping gesture with her hands. Seth's back sagged and he lowered his rifle, a broken, lost-spirited man. And the silent spoken curses began anew.

Billy Joe and Buck closed in on the homestead on foot, Buck professionally taking in the setup before him. One man holding a girl, another raider covering Seth and his wife standing on their stoop, with a rifle. And another three of the assholes coming out of the brush at the far side of the shack. 'A tricky situation, Billy Joe,' he muttered out of the side of his mouth. 'That little fat bastard who's got hold of the girl has a big Bowie at her throat. If we goin' to do something to change the situation there we'll have to do it real fast or that kid's dead.'

Billy Joe found himself having no inhibitions now about killing a man. The knife at the girl's throat vividly showed him how it must have been for his ma and sisters. He felt somehow he had acquired a divine right to see to it that suchlike scum stopped breathing the same air as decent, law-abiding folk.

'I'll take that sonuvabitch with the knife and his three buddies behind him, Sergeant,' he said softly, without taking his eyes off the group of men he intended throwing down on. 'You can take

on the other fella. Like you say, we'll do it right
now before they get over their surprise at us
showing up and start shooting. OK?'

Buck gave Billy Joe a sidelong glance of
amazement. Was the kid making a bad joke? He
could see no signs of humour on the skin-drawn,
tight face, still staring ahead at the scene at the
shack. Or of a blowhard over-estimating his
capabilities.

Keen to waste no more time Buck said, 'We'll do
it as you say, Billy Joe. You do the honours and I'll
send that target of mine winging on his way to
hell.'

Billy Joe's Henry came up from being held
across his chest and into his right shoulder, the
first shot shattering the knife-man's shoulder,
breaking his grip on the girl. The second shell
kicked up a small spiral of dust on his chest
pushing him further back from the girl almost
before the knife, dropping from fingers that had
lost strength to grip, bounced on the ground. Billy
Joe didn't waste another shell on him, didn't
waste any more time to see him hit the dirt, dead.

The firing of the fourteen remaining loads
sounded like one continuous roar. The deadly
leaden hail swept chest-high across the three
closing-in fast raiders cutting them down like
ripened corn under the scythe before they could
aim and fire their own guns. Buck played his part
by putting another eye, dark-blood-rimmed and
unseeing, in his target, sending him on the road to

hell as he had promised Billy Joe. And the small battle at the Bishops' shack was over, before the echoes of it had died away.

Buck and Billy Joe strode forward, Buck holding his rifle loosely in his left hand, right hand fisting his pistol. Billy Joe expertly thumbing a whole tube of reloads into the Henry. Mollie had rushed, sobbing loudly, into her mother's arms. Seth had picked up his rifle and was hurrying towards the three raiders on the killing ground to make sure that the trio were no longer a threat.

Buck grinned at Billy Joe. 'I must admit that I had doubts that you could do what you said but I stand corrected. I've never seen such fast and accurate shootin' with a long gun and, believe me, I've been around.'

Billy Joe's bony face softened somewhat in a slight smile. 'My pa said that was all I was good at, shootin' at targets with the old Henry. Though till a coupla days ago I hadn't shot at men before.'

Billy Joe's jaw tightened, the smile going as he noticed the girl's blood-marked hands, the slashed and hogshit smeared levis more than he did the pale, wild-eyed face. For the humiliation alone the raiders had made the girl suffer the sons-of-bitches deserved killing all over again.

Mollie drew away from her mother's comforting embrace when she saw the solemn-faced young man eyeing her. She looked down at her fouled and torn pants and her face flamed with embarrassment. 'Oh Ma!' she sobbed, and ran into the house.

Mrs Bishop smiled at them. 'Thank the Lord for your coming along in time, Sergeant Taylor, and you too, young man. I take it that you're a Ranger as well.' Then the terrible thoughts of how things could have turned out showed in her face and a flood of tears dampened down her welcoming smile.

'No Billy Joe here ain't a Ranger, ma'am,' Buck replied. 'But he has a very special reason for riding along with me. And I reckon we're all pleased that he did so.'

'Amen to that,' Mrs Bishop said, drying her tears with the edge of her apron. With her smile once more on her face she said, 'I'm neglecting my duty as a plainswoman, Sergeant Taylor. I'll go and fix some vittles for you and Billy Joe.' She glanced down at the raider Buck had killed, practically at her feet. She shuddered and her smile became a fixed mirthless grimace. 'I suppose you men will have some unfinished business to do. Come inside when it's done.'

Seth came back from checking on the three raiders, burdened with their rifles and pistol belts. He dumped them in a heap on the porch then smiled admiringly at Billy Joe. 'All dead, friend, well and truly so. I take it it was a 'fire-all-week' Henry you were using. Ain't seen one of them in action since the war.'

'Seth, meet Mr Billy Joe Foy,' Buck said. 'The

fastest *hombre* with a rifle in the territory bar none.'

'I'll second that opinion, Buck,' replied Seth. 'And me and my family will always be beholden to you, Mr Foy.' The homesteader's face hardened and pointed with his chin to the two nearest bodies. 'I suppose we'll have to see to them though it goes against the grain to see comancheros, they have the cut of that murderous breed, buried on my land.'

'Tarp them up and sling them across their horses,' Buck told him. 'Me and Billy Joe will take them with us when we ride out. There's plenty of rocks in Dead Horse Canyon to see them reasonably planted.' He grinned at Seth and Billy Joe. 'It ain't as though they're Christian-minded *hombres*, believing in real burials, hymn singing, preacher readin' over them and flowers.'

'That's OK by me, Buck,' Seth said, gratefully. 'Let's get it done then we can get washed up then go inside and eat. I take it Lill is preparing some chow?'

'I'll stay out on watch, Sergeant Taylor,' Billy Joe said. 'These fellas lying here could be part of a bigger bunch that right now could be wondering what has happened to them.' That wasn't the real excuse for Billy Joe not wanting to go inside the house. He didn't know if he could take sitting down at a table and eating with a family so soon after losing his without showing himself up in front of the Bishops by dashing out in case he started to bawl like an hysterical girl.

Buck saw Seth opening his mouth to protest but guessing Billy Joe's reason for his offering to stand guard said, 'Good thinkin', Billy Joe. And being the handiest man with a rifle among the three of us you're the best one for the chore. Now let's get these sonsuvbitches parcelled up, Seth, then we can partake of that chow your good lady wife is preparing for us so I can get back to my boys before they start worrying about me.' Po-faced he added, 'They ain't done so up till now but one day they might find it in their stone-hard hearts to fret about me in my absence.'

As the table was being prepared for the meal, Buck told the Bishops of how Billy Joe had met up with his patrol and about his one-man vendetta against Don Jose and his gang for massacring his family. Sombre-faced the Bishops listened, knowing how dangerously near they had been to suffering the same fate. Their sympathetic thoughts went out to Billy Joe, Mrs Bishop and Mollie openingly weeping.

'I reckon,' Buck concluded, 'why the kid didn't want to sit down and eat with us was that he hasn't come to terms yet with him being all that's left of his family. He'll kinda feel guilty that he's been spared. So he's atoning for it by trying to kill the Don. Or, more than likely, the way he intends goin' about it, get himself killed.'

Mrs Bishop only laid enough food on the table for her husband and Buck. 'Me and Mollie will eat

later,' she said. 'I'm fixing up a tray for Billy Joe,
and Mollie wants to take it out to him.'

Billy Joe sat on a box in the shadow of a barn on
the edge of Seth Bishop's land, eagle-eyeing the
belt of thick brush in front of him. If further
trouble came he judged that it would come from
there. He was far enough from the house to be
able, if he could hold them back for a spell, to give
Mr Bishop and Sergeant Taylor sufficient warning of the attack for them to prepare some sort of
defence.

In the barn Billy Joe heard the snorting and
hoof-stamping of the *comancheros'* horses, the
dead owners, lying in a line on the floor, tarp and
rawhide lashed, keeping a silent vigil, waiting
patiently for their final ride. Just a few days ago,
thought Billy Joe, he hadn't seen a body of a man
who had met his end violently. Now the dead were
piling up behind him. He saw again the frightened
faces of Mollie Bishop and her ma. His lips
thinned. Their lives were worth more than a
whole mountain of *comanchero* corpses.

Billy Joe heard a slight noise and turned his
head to see Mollie Bishop coming slowly towards
him carrying a tray holding a coffee jug and
dishes that chinked and rattled every step she
took. He laid the Henry on the ground and got to
his feet, stepping forward to relieve her of the
heavily laden tray.

'Ma's made you a hot meal and some fresh
coffee, Mr Foy,' Mollie said. Then, plucking up her

courage she added, 'I've brought food for myself as
well. I'd like to sit out here and eat it with you,
that's if you don't mind my company?'

Mollie didn't think that she was acting a mite
too pushy. It seemed only natural for her to get
closer to a boy who, at risk to his own life, had
saved hers. He would be riding out soon, probably
she would never see him again, then it would be
too late to thank him for coming to her rescue.
And, she thought, talking to him might, for a
while at least, take his mind off thinking about
what had happened to his own family. It was as
her ma had said, Mr Billy Joe Foy was too young
to have those shadows and lines on his face.

Billy Joe took in the fresh, smooth-skinned face,
the wide blue eyes gazing expectantly at him, the
tight at the waist, cornflower-coloured dress
showing the round firmness of her breasts to the
full. And the sweet smell of her perfume. Miss
Mollie Bishop sure looked a heap prettier than
when he had first seen her.

'Why I'd be delighted with your company, Miss
Bishop,' he said. He stood there, gawking at her
beauty like the back-country hick he was, holding
the tray, wondering where they could sit and eat.
Well away from the barn and its grisly tenants.

'Over there on the ridge, Mr Foy,' Mollie said.
'Under that lone oak. It's cool and shady there. It's
my favourite picnic spot.'

Billy Joe grinned and Mollie caught a fleeting
glimpse of the young Mr Foy as he had once been.

'OK, Miss Bishop, the ridge it is then.'

'Your ma is a good cook, Miss Bishop,' Billy Joe
said as Mollie poured out the last of the coffee into
his cup, a wafer-thin china cup so fragile that he
hardly dare grip the handle in case he snapped it
off. 'And I ain't seen such fancy cups before let
alone drink out of one.'

'Ma's special set,' Mollie said. 'Only brought out
for birthday parties, close kinsfolk weddings.' She
was going to say funerals as well but there had
been enough real deaths on the farm today. 'It was
my grandma's. She brought it with her all the way
from Baltimore. By wagon-train from St Louis. It
was her wedding present from her ma and pa.'
Mollie sweet-smiled at him. 'And call me Mollie.
Miss Bishop makes me feel as though I'm an old
maid.'

Billy Joe, looking at the brush, still watching
out for possible threats, said, softly, 'My ma was a
good cook.' He swung round and faced Mollie,
smiling nostalgically. Again Mollie saw Billy Joe
as he should be. Then he shifted his gaze back on
to the brush once more and Mollie saw his
jaw-line stiffen. As little as Mollie knew of the
complicated, sometimes contradictory, workings
of someone's mind she opined that it would take a
great deal of time before Billy Joe's mind was
cleared of all its turmoil, allowing him to take up
his own life again.

Impulsively she leant over and kissed a

surprised Billy Joe on the cheek. 'Billy Joe,' she said, 'you're a good man. Thanks for giving me my life back. And if you ever come by this way again on your travels you pay us a call, promise?' Billy Joe got another blood-stirring smile. 'Then I'll ask ma to get her special coffee set out again.'

Billy Joe couldn't promise. It wasn't in his hands to make such a commitment. Don Jose Valiente was running his life now. Yet he didn't want to falsely build up Mollie's hopes so all he said was, 'I'll see.' And left it at that.

Mollie didn't really expect any other answer. God, she firmly believed, had brought Billy Joe to this particular spot in Texas for a specific purpose. That purpose had been carried out; she was still alive. Mollie glanced fearfully at the barn. And that purpose had been carried out with all the destruction of life of an Old Testament prophecy. Now Billy Joe had to follow his chosen path and she had no part in it. Though, Mollie thought, it would have been nice to have met up with Billy Joe in more pleasant circumstances, m'be at a hoedown or church meeting-house dance. It seemed to Mollie that being sparked-up to, or the hopeful possibility of it, by a presentable boy was not to come her way. She would, she thought dolefully, be feeding hogs till she was a dried-juiced old maid.

'It's time I was going back, Billy Joe, to help ma to clear up,' Mollie said, and began to load the tray with the dirty crockery.

'I'll come with you,' Billy Joe said, taking the tray out of her hands. 'Sergeant Taylor will be wanting to make Dead Horse Canyon before dark.' He left it to Mollie to guess what for. It was a chore he wasn't looking forward to doing.

Mollie picked up the Henry and, for a moment or two before she followed him down from the ridge, she felt its lethal weight, wondering how many times Billy Joe would have to use it before he got peace of mind. Or, she thought despondently, as Sergeant Taylor had told her pa, got himself killed.

They were mounted up, ready to ride out. The horses carrying the dead men were tied together by a single lead rope tied to Buck's saddle-horn.

'You're sure you'll be OK, Seth?' Buck asked. 'I ain't too happy about leavin' you on your own but as soon as I catch up with the herd I'll send two of the boys back here. They can spend a coupla days scoutin' around just to make certain everything's OK.' Buck smiled at Mrs Bishop. 'Now don't you fill them up with that good chow you cook or I'll never get them back.'

'We'll be OK till then, Buck,' Seth replied, putting his arm round his wife's shoulders. 'Me and Ma have had to defend our home against Injun raids when we first came here.'

Billy Joe saw Mrs Bishop's and Mollie's worried, anxious looks, mirroring, he knew, what Mr Bishop was feeling but for his family's sake

dare not show. His pa must have had the same
gut-shrivelling feelings when hearing of neighbours being raided. But he'd had a son to share his
fears with, another rifle to defend the women.

'I'll stay, Sergeant,' he said. 'I'll come with you
as far as the canyon, help you to do what's to be
done there, then ride back here. If Mr Bishop
don't object to me sleeping in his barn and Mrs
Bishop don't mind feeding me. And it's OK with
you of course.'

Billy Joe didn't have to ask if it was OK with the
Bishops, he could read it in their relieved smiles.

'You needn't send another man back, Buck,'
Seth said. 'We've got four rifles now and I won't be
caught off guard again if trouble comes.'

Billy Joe volunteering to stay on at the holding
suited Buck fine though he didn't tell Billy Joe
why. He had been working on a plan to put to the
captain that would take the fight against the Don
into the son-of-a-bitch's backyard. Though he
reckoned that the captain wouldn't look on it as a
plan but as a harebrained, mad-assed scheme.
Whatever the captain's views on it if he could be
talked round to letting him go ahead with it he
would need Billy Joe's assistance. His handling of
the Henry could enable them to shorten the odds
of what Buck admitted was a long-odds chance of
his plan succeeding. And, more important, both of
them being alive at the end of it. Here, with the
Bishops, Billy Joe wouldn't be risking his life
patrolling on his lonesome along the Rio Grande.

For without Bill Joe's involvement in his plan he had no plan at all. Billy Joe was the only man who had the burning reason to ride with him no matter how crazy his plan seemed.

'Yeah that's OK, Billy Joe,' he said. 'I'll sell those spare horses of yours in El Paso. I should be riding this way with a full patrol in three, four days time, I'll settle up with you then.' He touched his hat in a farewell gesture at Mrs Bishop and Mollie then jerking at the lead rope said, 'Let's be moving out, Billy Joe, and get rid of these *hombres.*'

FOUR

'You must be *loco*, Sergeant,' Captain Sinclair said, 'to go into Mexico with only one man to seek out that murderin' bastard's hideout. Is there another crazy sonuvabitch in the company?'

Buck had reported in at Ranger HQ in El Paso; saw to it that the herd brands were checked for ownership against known Texas ranchers' brands. Then he gave orders to Cassidy to sell Billy Joe's horses, warning him of extra duties if he didn't get top price for them. All he had to do now before he signed off duty was to try and convince Captain Sinclair of the viability of his grand plan. It wouldn't be easy. The captain was a hard-nosed, veteran Ranger. In 1847 he served in a Ranger company fighting alongside Gen. Zachary Scot in the Mexican war.

Buck innocent-eyed his captain. 'I remember a certain Ranger captain who crossed the border and took back a herd of stolen Texas longhorns from a bunch of Mex cattle-lifters.'

'Yeah ... well ... I,' blustered Captain Sinclair.

'It was only a trip of eight, ten miles into Mex
territory and I had half a company of Rangers
with me. And it was only a few ragged-assed Mex
cattle thieves we were jumping. The Don runs a
small army, controls northern Chihuahua. He'll
know that two *gringos* have crossed the Rio
Grande before you've got clear of the shallows.'
Captain Sinclair shook his head chidingly. 'What
with him and his wild-assed *muchachos* and the
likelihood of meeting up with a *rurale* patrol you'll
never get the chance to do any snooping around.'

'The beauty of my plan, Capt'n,' Buck said
patiently, 'is that I don't intend walking into the
Don's front parlour. I'm coming on to the
Candelarias from Sonora. I don't think the Don
operates west of the mountains so I should have
no trouble in getting in real close to try and pick
up signs of his whereabouts. The big bunch of men
he leads oughta leave some tracks to follow.' Buck
didn't tell the captain that more than likely
Sonora could also have its *bandido gringo*-haters.
So it could turn out to be anything but a peaceful
ride across the State of Sonora. To be truthful to
himself the more he talked about his plan the
more he thought that the captain was right about
him being *loco*. Still trying to sound confident he
said, 'It's a chance, Capt'n, m'be a wild one. But
it's better than poundin' our asses along the
border tryin' and failin' to stop the Don comin'
across.'

Captain Sinclair fiddled idly with some papers

on his desk, thinking that his first opinion of his sergeant's scheme now that he had heard it all was still valid, wild crazy though it was. Yet he couldn't come up with another plan to put an end to the Don's raiding. He and his Rangers were coming in for a lot of shit from the ranchers and farmers along the border for not protecting them. Buck's plan, when it came down to bare-assed facts, was the only option he had. That didn't mean that he was keen for Buck to ride out in the so-called line of duty to commit suicide.

'If I give you the go-ahead, Buck,' he said sourly, 'this Ranger you intend takin', is he up to the job?'

Buck grinned inwardly. He had swung the captain to his way of thinking. 'He sure is, Capt'n. Though he ain't a Ranger, leastways not yet he ain't. But I've every intention of seeing he becomes one before we cross the Rio Grande.'

Captain Sinclair raised his eyebrows in surprised disbelief at the thought of Buck taking along an untrained civilian with him on such a dangerous mission. 'He'd better be good, Buck,' he growled. 'It's your neck that's on the block.'

Buck then told the captain about Billy Joe, the raid on his pa's farm, the killing of his family and his one-man mission to kill the Don. And of the shootings at Seth Bishop's holding. 'He's good under pressure, Capt'n. Handles a rifle better than any man I've met or heard of. The kid's already been across the line, seen off four of the Don's boys and brought a bunch of rustled Texas longhorns back. No, Capt'n I ain't worried about taking him along as my pard.'

Captain Sinclair still wasn't entirely won over with Buck's choice of partners. 'He'll have to be watched,' he warned Buck. 'With all the hate he must be feeling against the Don he could force you into taking mad-assed risks and chances.'

Buck grinned at Captain Sinclair. 'I will, because I sure ain't hankerin' to be another "Glory Boy" General Custer.'

'OK then, you do it, Buck,' the captain said. 'And the best of luck to you both. If you do strike paydirt, find out where the Don spends his leisure-time, you come ass-kicking back here *pronto*, savvy?' He favoured Buck with a hard-eyed bossman's look.

'That's exactly what I had in mind, Capt'n,' replied Buck, all choirboy-innocent again. 'As I said I ain't lookin' for glory.'

'Make sure that you don't forget that,' Captain Sinclair said, 'because I intend to haul-ass off this chair and lead the company myself across the Rio Grande and personally shoot down, or hang that murderin' Mex sonuvabitch.'

Billy Joe heard Seth call out the ominous words, 'Riders comin' in!' He put down the feed pail, picked up the Henry and, dropping the holding bar of the corral gate, hurried across to the house, hard and old-looking visaged, warily watching the moving dust haze along the trail. Mollie and her mother were standing alongside Seth on the porch, frightened-eyed, holding each other's hands for mutual comfort and support.

As Billy Joe stepped on to the porch, Seth, shielding his eyes from the high-noon glare, smiled. 'It's OK, folks, it's Buck with a Ranger patrol.'

Mollie let go of her mother's hand and, smiling at Billy Joe, stepped closer to him. Billy Joe felt her cool fingers grip and squeeze his hand and held it as the riders rode up to the house. His face lost its uncompromising Indian-eyed look as suddenly he knew that there could be a life for him, if he was still alive that is, after he had settled up with the Don. That thought he now knew had been unconsciously developing during the four days he had spent with the Bishops.

He was finding that he was becoming less screwed up inside, being fussed over, over-fed by Mrs Bishop and sleeping in a proper bed, Seth insisting that good friends of the Bishops don't bed down with critters. Plus the good feelings he was getting by being with Mollie. The anger against the Don and the determination to put paid to him were still there but now under control, realizing, as Sergeant Taylor had hinted, that it would take more than foolhardy courage to take on, and win, his war against the Don.

The good feelings were not just running one way, Mollie was also aware of similar pleasant stirrings inside her. For a young girl, feeling the burning urges and desires of blossoming

womanhood, life on the open plains was a lonely,
frustrating existence. The only time Mollie met
people of her own age were the weekly Sunday
church meetings and the occasional barn dance, at
both events being chaperoned by her parents. Even
at the dances she only had the freedom to exchange
giggling whispered fantasies to other girls about
boys who could turn out to be their future hus-
bands. Romance was a wet-mouthed kiss; hot,
hasty hands fumbling at her breasts were just as
swiftly brushed aside, in the darkness of the brush
behind the barn.

Now, thought Mollie, she'd had a boy all to herself
for almost four days, albeit a boy whose destiny was
etched deeply in his hard-eyed face, whose future
she already knew didn't include normal boy and girl
relationships. But that didn't deter Mollie from
indulging in a spot of wishful thinking of how things
might have turned out for her.

They had been up on the ridge twice since the
first day, Billy Joe always carrying his deadly rifle.
Though relaxed enough when they sat down to talk
a little about his family, she hadn't the courage to
reach out then to take his hand in hers. Not, she
admitted, a gesture of blazing, unbridled passion
but a further breaking of the ice between them.
Only now on the porch, when Billy Joe would soon
be riding out of her life forever, had she reached out
to him, and got an encouraging response in return.

The troop rode past the house in a drifting
billow of dust, carrying on to the foot of the ridge

before halting. Buck had peeled off and dismounted in front of the porch, noticing as he did so Billy Joe letting go of Mollie Bishop's hand. He gave a low grunt of satisfaction. The kid was mellowing. He wanted him mean and angry for the task ahead of them but he didn't want him to end up as a mean-assed drifter, following no star, no good as a Ranger and as sure as hell, no good to himself.

Buck raised his hat to the ladies then asked Seth if it was OK for his boys to water their horses at his trough.

'You tell them to help themselves, Buck,' replied Seth. 'Mollie, help your ma to get some coffee brewin'.'

'We're goin' to give the territory a good goin' over, Seth,' Buck said. 'Flush out any *comancheros* who may be hangin' around lookin' for easy pickin's. I don't think there is but the capt'n says we've got to make sure and he's the man that gives out the orders. Corporal Cassidy will be leadin' the patrol. I've business elsewhere.' He looked directly at Billy Joe, handing him a tight roll of dollar bills. 'Cass got you the best price he could for your horses, Billy Joe. Before you spend it to grubstake yourself for your fight against the Don I've a proposition to put to you. Being that we both want the Don dead I opine that we should pair up. I have a sorta plan which could get the result you want faster than prowlin' along the Rio Grande waiting for the sonuvabitch to show his face. Are you interested?'

'I'm interested in any plan that will get me

within rifle range of the Don, Sergeant Taylor,'
Billy Joe said flatly.

Buck smiled. 'I was bankin' on you being so
inclined, Billy Joe.'

Billy Joe was saying his goodbyes to the Bishops,
shaking Seth's hand, getting a kiss on the cheek
from Mrs Bishop, and an embrace and a kiss on
the lips from a tearful Mollie. A red-faced,
thoughtful Billy Joe heaved himself into his
saddle. Seth, Mrs Bishop and Buck trying hard
not to smile. Buck said, 'Let's go!'

Billy Joe followed him for five or six yards then
suddenly swung his mount round to pull up
alongside the porch again. He looked down, stern-
faced, at Mollie. 'I intend coming back this way,
Miss Bishop,' he said. 'That's if you want me to.'

Mollie beamed then burst into tears and ran
into the house. Seth grinned at the puzzled-
looking Billy Joe. 'That means yes, Billy Joe. Now
you and Buck take care, do you hear?'

'I will, Mr Bishop,' Billy Joe said and, pulling
away, knee'd Jubla in the flanks and caught up
with Buck.

Buck thought disappointedly that he had lost
out in making Billy Joe into a Ranger. Hard-
assing it all over Texas, being shot at by *bandidos*,
white, red and brown was a poor alternative to a
life with a pretty wife, unless the *hombre* was as
crazy as he had been twenty-five years ago when
he had upped and joined the Rangers.

FIVE

'I've never been in this part of Mexico before, Billy Joe,' Buck said dourly. 'Though I reckon it ain't no different to the parts I've visited. That just over the next rise there could be mean-minded, taking *hombres*, willing to beat our heads in for the fine leather *gringo* boots we're wearin'. What hurt they would inflict on us for our horses and the gear the two burros are carryin' don't bear thinkin' about.'

They had slipped across the border from New Mexico, east of the border town of Agve Prieta, Billy Joe up on a real horse for greater speed, keeping clear of villages and settlements; not wanting the news of two *gringos*, well worth robbing to reach the ears of men who classed killing and robbing of travellers as a normal way of earning their keep, and, most of all, to the ears of the most dangerous thief of them all, Don Jose Valiente. Somewhere, if Buck was right in his reasoning, on the other side of the dark jagged-outlined ridges of the Candelarias coming into view on their left.

'We'll move on to the mountains now,' Buck said. 'Cut through them then start lookin' for tracks. I opine that the Don's hole-up won't be too far south of the Rio Grande. He'll not want to ride across half of Chihuahua and risk bumpin' into a Mexican Army or *rurale* patrol.' He cold-smiled Billy Joe. 'This is where the goin' could get tough. Those hills up ahead are the happy huntin' grounds of wild-assed Apache and Yaqui. They could stop fightin' each other long enough for them to partake in the delights of liftin' two white eyes' hair.'

Closing in on the mountains, as the ground began to rise into the foothills, Buck and Billy Joe came across a well-used trail that cut into the mountains after rounding a rocky spur.

'It seems a likely way through, Billy Joe,' Buck said. 'Though we could meet up with *hombres* comin' through the pass from Chihuahua and we don't want to show ourselves if we can avoid it. We'll scout around for a higher trail. That oughta keep our presence unseen. Stop any likely bushwhacker from shootin' down on us.'

The faint blaze of the track they finally discovered ran up the ridge of the rocky spur, dog-legged its tortuous way around a towering, split-faced black butte before heading in the same easterly direction as the wide, rock-strewn canyon the used trail led into. The track presented no problem to the two sure-footed burros but Buck and Billy Joe dismounted and rein-led their horses rather than stay in the saddle and risk a neck-breaking fall to the floor of the canyon.

Suddenly, from beyond the next twist in the track, they heard the echoing rattle of gunfire. As near, as Buck quickly calculated, to ten rifles. Exchanging significant glances they tied the animals to tufts of brush sprouting out of the cracks in the butte's face and, drawing their rifles, went forward on foot.

Looking down on the small battle, Buck noted that he had guessed more or less right the size of it. Six rifles in a line across the full width of the canyon were firing on three guns positioned in the rocks on the side of the canyon facing them. Two bodies lay in the dust between the two factions. Buck, using his army glasses, took a closer look to see just who the protagonists were.

The three rifles were Apache. Crouching deeper in the rocky tumble were five more Apache, women and children. Buck swept his glasses over the men who had the Apache boxed in. With the glasses still to his eyes he said, 'We won't be able to sneak by them, Billy Joe. Both sides will cut loose at us thinkin' that we're reinforcements for the other; pick us off like flies on a wall. We'll have to take sides and end this fight or go back and try and find another trail.'

'Whose side do we join, Buck?' Billy Joe asked.

Buck lowered his glasses and turned and faced Billy Joe. 'There's five longhorns at the back of those six riflemen so the way I read it the Apache down there have been caught by the balls liftin' someone's beef. As those *hombres* are too well armed up to be honest, hard-working *vaqueros* your guess is as good as mine who's the owner of the cattle and who those sonsuvbitches ride for.'

'Are they some of the Don's murdering scum?' Billy Joe said.

'Could well be or some other *bandido*'s wild-assed boys,' replied Buck. 'One thing's for sure, they ain't cowhands. If we back them we'll have odds of three to one to face if they turn nasty. There's only three Apache, even-steven odds. We'll have a better chance of making it a Mexican standoff with them should they come out on top and still fancy roastin' us over a slow fire. And, further more, one of those dead Apache is a woman and I don't hold with the gunnin' down of females, whatever colour.' He grinned at Billy Joe. 'I never thought the day would come when I would fight alongside the Apache. Being that you're a dead-eyed Dick, Billy Joe, you take the fella furthest away and work in over. Between us and the Apache we should send them hell-bound.'

Billy Joe drew a bead on the boulder behind which his first target was sheltering. He saw the ragged top of a high-crowned hat come slowly into view, then a swarthy, straggling moustached profile as the Mexican sighted his rifle on the Apache. Billy Joe pulled off one shell and what had been a face before the heavy slug ripped its way through and out of it in a welter of blood, disappeared from his sight again.

Being that he had only the lower part of one leg to aim at it took Billy Joe two shots to send the second Mexican winging on his way to hell to meet up with his *compadre*. The whole of the upper part of the Mexican's body heaved upright in an automatic, shock spasm reaction to the nerve-shredding agony of a shattered kneecap, presenting Billy Joe with an easy shot. A split-second before he fired he saw the Mexican's body jerk violently backwards and guessed that one of the Apache had fired a killing shot as well.

Buck's contribution in the small battle was to send two more of the enemy sprawling lifeless on the ground. The last two, realizing that they were under unexpected and deadly, flanking fire, took action to save their skins. One twisted round and began to fire at the new threat to his life. Billy Joe, accepting Buck's reasoning that the man killed and raped for the Don, calmly and dispassionately put two loads into him, as close together in the region of his heart as a man showing off his firing skills on a shooting-range would hole an ace card.

The sole survivor lacked the balls to continue the fight when the odds had suddenly turned against him. Chickening out he stood up and made a weaving, ducking run for his horse, only getting a few yards in his panicky bid to save his skin when a fusillade of shells, white eye and

Apache, struck him in the back. The speeding bullets' momentum forced along a near dead man in a drunk's stumbling run till he folded at the knees and fell face down in the dust.

The sounds of the firing were still bouncing around the high peaks when Buck got to his feet and laid down his rifle. As further proof to the Apache of his peaceful intentions he unbuckled his gunbelt, held it high for a moment or two, then laid it down beside his rifle. Billy Joe still lay prone with the Henry covering the three Apache, now standing clear of the rocks, straddled-legged, rifles held across their chest, looking up at them. His eyes caught movement behind the Apache riflemen and he saw the women and the children picking their way down to the floor of the canyon. The women hurried over to the two dead Apache. He heard their high keening wails of grief as they knelt down by the bodies. The children ran past them, the older ones making sure that the Mexicans were really dead and collecting their guns. Billy Joe saw the sun flash off a knife blade. He shuddered. The Apache were collecting a victor's trophy. The Mexicans would have been doing likewise if they had come out on top, and been paid a bounty by their government for their trouble. The other children were rounding up the Mexicans' horses and the four longhorns. And still the three Apache stood, rock-still, eyeing Buck standing just as rigid.

'I'll have to go down and have a talk with those

bare-assed gents,' Buck said.

'Ain't that a bit risky?' Billy Joe replied. 'Being unarmed and all?'

'Darned hairy I'd say,' answered Buck. 'But those fellas could probably tell us more about the Don's whereabouts than you and me would find out in weeks of hard-assin' along these ridges. I've heard that the Apache are men of honour, beholden to *hombres* who do them a good deed. We've just pulled them out of a tight corner so I reckon that they owe us, Billy Joe.' Buck pointed to his right. 'That seems a likely place for an old fart like me to get down to those Apache without me breakin' my neck.' He looked down at Billy Joe. 'But just in case our red brothers ain't filled with the milk of human kindness I'd appreciate it if you'd keep your old Henry's sights on them. If things ain't goin' my way I'll take my hat off and whether I get back up here again will depend on your fast and accurate shootin'.'

Billy Joe looked up at Buck, trying not to show his nervousness. On his own, only his life was in forfeit against the accuracy of his shooting. Now Buck was giving him the awful responsibility of putting his life in his hands. He gripped the Henry with grim determination. 'You go down and have your pow-wow, Buck, I'll watch out for you.'

Below him, Billy Joe heard the sounds of dislodged rocks rattling down to the valley floor, followed by Buck's loud cursing. He grinned, feeling more confident. The old goat didn't let

anything put him off from acting normally. If it
had been his choice to pick a man to ride with him
against the Don he couldn't have chosen a better
hombre than Sergeant Buckley Taylor.

Buck came into his view as he walked across the
canyon floor towards the three Apache, stopping a
few feet short of them. Billy Joe saw much arm
waving from Buck as he spoke to the Apache.
Making up, he surmised, for what he didn't know
the Apache word for. He also saw the brief flare of
a struck match. The Apache were men of honour
after all. One time Buck twisted round to point up
at him. The Apache raised their heads and
glanced in his direction then the four settled down
to continue with their talking.

Billy Joe relaxed and sat up, resting his rifle
easy across his knees, dividing his time between
keeping a watch on Buck and their new-found
friends and the women and children strapping
their meagre possessions onto four of the dead
Mexicans' horses, the other two horses already
burdened with the two Apache dead. To be taken,
opined Billy Joe, to wherever they intended giving
them their last rites, in the Apache way of doing
such things.

When all was ready the horses were led out,
following the cattle into a narrow canyon whose
mouth was part hidden by thick brush, leaving
only the Apache warriors' mounts and the now
naked and scalped bodies of the Mexicans. High
overhead, in the washed-out blue bowl of a sky,

black specks hovered on the rising thermals, watching, waiting. Joined all the while by more buzzards swooping down from the far ridges. Billy Joe shivered. He hoped to hell he wasn't getting a foresight into his and Buck's end.

The meeting finally broke up, the Apache going across to their horses, Buck walking to the canyon wall and his scramble back up to the track. Billy Joe saw two of the Apache ride away in a flurry of dust and stones, heading for the hidden side canyon. But he got to wondering why the third Apache was riding slowly eastwards, to Chihuahua, along the main trail.

He stood up and walked the few steps to the spot where Buck was climbing up. From well down the slope Billy Joe could hear Buck's laboured breathing, and his curses when he slipped back on the loose shale. Grinning, he stretched out a helping hand and when the crimson, sweat-streaked-faced Buck got within grabbing distance he clutched at it thankfully, allowing Billy Joe to yank him on to the track.

Buck lay on his back, chest heaving like a blown horse's flanks for several minutes before his breathing became regular enough for him to tell Billy Joe the outcome of his talks with the Apache.

'I was right,' he said. 'The Mexses' were some of the Don's *bandidos*. The Apache are Warm Spring Apache, reservation jumpers, on their way to meet up with Nana in the Sierra Madres. Got jumped on while helping themselves to a few of the Don's stolen cattle.' Buck raised himself on to his elbows. 'The red devils know where the Don's hole-up is. When I told them what the Don did to your family and you're huntin' him down, Chulo, he was the young one, offered to lead us to it. Like you he has a pressing reason for wanting to get real close to the Don. One of the Apache dead was his sister.'

Groaning, flexing his limbs, Buck struggled to his feet. 'Let's get movin', Billy Joe, before I seize up. Chulo's meetin' us along the trail, this track we're on drops down on to the main trail about a mile ahead.' Buck favoured Billy Joe with a wry, twisted grin. 'Now I'll tell you the bad news. The Don's got watchers out on the border crossin's so my great plan of the capt'n and the whole company fireballing across the Rio Grande and stompin' out a nest of rattlers has fallen through.'

Billy Joe eyeballed Buck angrily. 'Does that mean you're quitting?'

'No it don't!' snapped Buck. 'I wasn't just sweatin' my balls off climbin' this Goddamned hill, I also thought of another plan. We harass the Don as much as we can. Steal his beef, shoot down his boys if we can jump some of them. Make the sonuvabitch mad angry so that he calls in his watchers from the border to join in the huntin' down of us. That oughta give me the chance to get the Rangers across the river and down here without being spotted as me and the capt'n had originally planned.' He looked closely at Billy Joe to see if he could detect any signs of disagreement with his plan. Seeing none but realizing it wasn't the greatest of plans he said, 'I know it's a crazy, "Glory Boy" plan and my capt'n would bust me for even thinkin' of such a mad-assed scheme. But it's either that or us ridin' back to El Paso and report a failed mission. Of course Chulo will have to buy it. Without his Apache sneaky way of thinkin' and movin' around, me and you wouldn't be able to stop the Don and his boys from grabbin' us within a few hours in territory we don't know. And, of course, you being my pard, Billy Joe, if you think that the risk's not worth it we'll call the whole thing off.'

Billy Joe opined that Buck giving him the opportunity to quit was a way of telling him that he knew of his growing friendship with Miss Mollie Bishop. Thinking that m'be it had made him a mite more reluctant to take any more wild chances. He was thinking of Mollie Bishop too and of how pleasant life would be with her as his wife. But blood came first. Hardening his heart he said, 'My plan of riding along the border on my own wasn't exactly a piece of real logical thinking, Buck, but it didn't stop me from trying it out. It seemed the right thing to do at the time. We'll do as you say.' He gave Buck a lopsided, mirthless grin. 'It might all come right for two crazy sonsuvbitches.'

Buck smiled back at him. 'Let's go and see if our friend, Chulo, is as *loco*.'

SIX

Buck swore loudly and pulled up his mount and dismounted. 'I'll have to walk her, Billy Joe,' he said. 'Or that front leg she's lost the shoe off will go lame. I've got to find a village where I can get a new shoe fitted. If the Don's boys show up and I'm ridin' a horse that can't move no faster than a slow walk then our harassment of the Don will end there and then, permanently. We'll be well and truly dead.'

Chulo had led them out of the canyon and was trailing them south, though still keeping close to the foothills. Chulo, riding well out on the flank, could give them plenty warning if he saw the raised dust cloud of riders for them to move deeper into the hills. The Don's canyon hideout, Chulo had told them, was twenty miles ahead but before they reached it they would have to go back into the mountains, trail up and over a ridge; then, if all went well, they would be gazing down into the Don's backyard.

Buck had introduced Billy Joe to Chulo when

they had met up on the floor of the canyon. Billy Joe took in a wiry-framed youth about his age, with a thin-lipped, bony face and an unblinking, cold-eyed stare that gave him the shakes. He was armed with an old single-shot horse soldier carbine, whose cracked stock was bound together by a piece of Western Union telegraph wire, and a big, naked-bladed knife stuck in a belt around his middle.

'You impressed Chulo, and his buddies with your shootin', Billy Joe,' Buck said. 'They told me that they had never seen a rifle fired so fast before, and bang on target.'

Billy Joe saw that Chulo was eyeing his rifle trying hard not to show a white eye's envious curiosity. Smiling Billy Joe handed the Henry over to Chulo to examine more closely. 'It's a rifle as old as yours, Chulo, but holds sixteen shots.' He didn't know if the Apache understood all he had said but Chulo's eyes lit up, ending the fearful Apache stare as he hefted the gun from one hand to another, feeling its weight and balance. He gave it back to Billy Joe with a grunted '*Bueno*' and the shutters cut off the light behind his eyes again.

Chulo joined them on the trail, unseen and unheard till he appeared alongside them, Billy Joe thinking as though he had just dropped out of the sky.

'Is there a village nearby, Chulo?' Buck said. 'If I don't get a new shoe on this horse's foot in no way will she be fit enough to climb those ridges.'

Chulo pointed to his left. 'One hour, village,' he replied.

'Fine,' said Buck. 'I ain't too happy about us openly showing ourselves to some Mex villagers, the Don's bound to have spies scattered around hereabouts, but when we light that fire under the Don's ass I want to be able to move faster than an old fart like me can shift on two feet. I reckon it'll be wiser for me to go in on my own.' He grinned at Billy Joe and Chulo. 'Of course I'm expecting you young bloodthirsty bucks to hang about nearby in case I get into trouble.'

They stopped when they could see the village's whitewashed mission bell-tower shimmering in the baking heat. Buck asked Chulo to check out the village to see if it was calm and peaceful enough for a lone *gringo* to ride in and out again, all in one piece.

Not till he had heard the faint chink of stone against stone from beyond the bend in the *arroyo* in which he and Buck were sheltering, did Billy Joe know that Chulo had returned from his scouting out of the village. Seeing his startled-looking face Buck grinned. 'The kid kinda moves around real quiet, don't he?'

'I'm glad he was willing to come in on your plan, Buck,' Billy Joe said. 'Two *gringos*, heavy-footing across what rightly could be enemy territory, would be taking one helluva risk before the war had really got started.'

Chulo reported that the village was as peaceful as it looked. There were tracks of eight iron-shod horses entering the village from along the mountain trail, then leaving northwards to the Rio Grande. That had been at least two days ago. Buck put the riders down as a bunch of the Don's men having the pleasure of a village woman or a last drink before riding to relieve their *compadres* on watch along the border. It gave him the chance to sneak into the village and get his horse seen to before the guards were changed again, or so he hoped.

Buck gave his final orders to his men. 'It seems that I should have no problems getting in and out but if I do run into trouble don't come running in to help me out unless you boys think you can handle it.' Buck fierce-eyed them. *'Comprende?'* Billy Joe nodded his head, lyingly. Chulo couldn't understand what the old *gringo* was talking about. If he had it would not have made any difference. He would endeavour to get within killing distance of the Don no matter what odds he could be called on to face. He had a lot more hate driving him on than Billy Joe. The Apache and the Mexicans had been killing each other for hundreds of years.

No one, not even curious children, showed themselves to Buck as he led his horse and one of the burros past a straggle of pockmarked-walled adobe houses. It might, thought Buck, have been

a village of the dead for the lack of interest it took
in a lone *gringo* stranger. But he knew that
unseen eyes from behind windows were watching
him. His coming into the village could later be
reported to the Don. At this stage in the game,
Buck didn't think that the Don would lose any
sleep over the news that one *gringo* with a laden
burro was in his bailiwick. Some of his *muchachos*
might think otherwise. Men, who, he opined,
would rob their own grandmothers, would take a
delight in relieving him of his horse and burro,
killing him in the process with as much delight.
Buck told himself that he was worrying like a
frightened old maid. It wasn't the first time as a
Texas Ranger he had gone out on a limb.

A larger building, outside of which stood two
mules, ears and tails flickering nonstop to ward
off pestering flies, Buck took to be the village
cantina. Its owner, if he wasn't asleep along with
the rest of the villagers, would be able to tell him
if there was a smithy nearby. The sudden
breaking of the graveyard silence of the village by
the sound of iron clanging against iron saved
Buck the trouble of going into the *cantina* and
rousing the owner from his siesta.

To Buck's surprise the blacksmith was a big,
barn-door, wide-shouldered Negro. The smith,
just as taken aback by the sight of an unexpected
gringo customer, stayed the downward swing of
his hammer for a moment or two then let his arm
drop easily down by his side, thrusting the iron

bar he was working on back into the furnace.

'Welcome to San Pedro, stranger,' he said. 'You're the first American I've cast eyes on in ten years.' He gave Buck a beaming, all-toothed smile. 'I'm Josh; the bossman on the plantation I was a slave on didn't hold with us Nigras having a second name.' He put his hand out in greeting, the big smile still creasing his face. 'I reckon now that old Abe Lincoln freed the slaves before he was killed it's OK for a Nigra to shake hands with a white man on equal terms without the risk of him being lynched.'

Serious-faced Buck said, 'Mr Josh, I don't give a damn whether you're black and have two heads; if you fix my horse up with a new shoe I'll get down on my knees and kiss your ass. My name is Buck Taylor, I'm headin' for the Candelarias, I've heard there's pockets of gold along the higher ridges.' He gripped the big smith's massive hand in a firm handshake, noting as he did so the old scars of hand irons.

Josh's smile waned then vanished altogether. 'Mr Taylor you heard wrong. There ain't no gold there. There's Apache and Mexican *bandidos* running around those canyons.' The smith waved both of his arms in a wide expansive gesture. 'This whole territory is *bandido* country. I don't know how you made it this far without ending up losing your horses and gear, that's after your throat had been cut. I'm only allowed to live here because the big boss of the *bandidos*, a murderous sonuvabitch who calls himself Don Jose Valiente, knows I'm good at repairing his fancy saddles and shoeing the string of horses he owns.'

Buck didn't let it show in his face that he knew all about the Don and his activities. Wide-eyed innocent he said, 'What I know about this fair land, Mr Josh, whatever trail a man rides somewhere along it there'll be ill-disposed gents waiting to relieve him of his possessions.'

'Mr Taylor,' Josh said, schoolmarmish, 'there's bad-asses, genuine *mal hombres*, then there's Don Jose and his butchers. If I was cursed to be taken alive by the Apache or Don Jose I'd plump for the Apache. The Don, for a so-called Christian gentleman, sure takes a delight in hurtin' folk real bad. He has this village terrified. His men ride in here to take whatever woman they fancy.' The big smith shrugged his shoulders. 'But if you're keen to go and seek out that gold you're yearnin' for then that's your business and I'll apologize for stickin' my nose into something that don't concern me.' Josh's smile returned. 'But we *gringos* can't let these greasers get the better of us. You bring your horse in, Mr Taylor and I'll see to it. There's water out back if you want to give the burro a drink.'

'No apologies needed, Mr Josh,' replied Buck as he led his horse into the barn. 'A man would be right churlish not to listen to advice honestly given. I'll keep a special watch out for this Don whatsisname, and his fun-lovin' boys. If they catch up with me then you can put it down to a stubborn old man's foolish dream of findin' a crock of gold.'

Buck took only part of the load off the burro as it drank just in case he had to move out in a hurry. Behind him he could hear Josh hammering out a new shoe otherwise the village was as silent as it had been when he had first entered it. Somehow that didn't give him peace of mind, or stop the bristling of his hair at the nape of his neck. By what Josh had told him, the village being regularly visited by the Don's men seeking their pleasures, the quietness could well be the calm before the storm.

When the burro had drunk its fill he fully loaded it again, checking that all the gear was tightly roped on, then led it around to the front of the barn.

More than Buck's hair twitched at the sight of a Mexican, bowed down with the weight of a rifle and a big pistol and criss-crossed shell belts across his chest, relieving himself against the rear wall of the *cantina*. The Mexican, still pissing, twisted his head round at the sound of the burro's footsteps. Buck gave him a false cheery, '*Buenos dias, señor*', and got a fish-eyed look in return as the Mexican buttoned up his flies.

Once inside the barn he asked if the man was one of the Don's gang.

Josh, grim-faced, nodded. 'There's four more of the sonsuvbitches inside the *cantina*. I saw them pass the mouth of the alley when they rode in.

Your horse is ready, Mr Taylor; you get astride it and ride out *pronto*, north for the Rio Grande, forget all about that pot of gold you're after seekin'. They'll come wanderin' over here when the mood takes them then you'll be buzzard meat for sure.'

Billy Joe and Chulo saw the five men ride into the village and draw up their mounts outside the building with the two mules tied up and go inside. Like Buck, Billy Joe guessed that the building was a *cantina*. It was a firm realization not a guess that Buck had suddenly been placed in the middle of a lion's den. Though he couldn't as yet hear sounds of gunfire Billy Joe tapped Chulo on the shoulder, as an indication to the Apache that they should go to Buck's aid. It would be too late to do so if they waited for the shooting to start. Keeping a watchful gaze on the open doorway of the *cantina* Billy Joe and Chulo sped in a crouching run towards the village.

Buck stepped out of the barn and into big trouble; four of the Don's men were now standing outside the rear door of the *cantina*. He wasn't a man who prejudged another man's character by his looks. He had seen young, choirboy-faced boys calmly back-shoot men. But if he hadn't known that the men were the Don's *bandidos* he would have had no hesitation in cataloguing the men walking towards him, big, savage-toothed spurs jingling, as out and out killing men. Every line in their hard, cruel faces shouted it out.

Buck's throat dried up. The sons-of-bitches weren't closing in to sweet-talk to him. Though he hadn't a cat in hell's chance of beating the four *pistoleros* he would be damned if he was going to stand, all shit-scared, and let them shoot him down like a dog. He would try and take at least two of them with him to wherever he was bound for in his afterlife.

'Draw, Buck!' Billy Joe's shout from the corner of the cantina galvanized Buck into action. Taking advantage of the split-second edge Billy Joe's yell had given him by distracting the *bandidos'* attention from him to Billy Joe, his hand flew downwards to his pistol.

The Mexican who had earlier been relieving his bladder staggered back a pace as though he had bumped into an invisible wall, then dropped forward, straight and true like a felled tree to show a big jagged, bloody, shell exit hole in the back of his coat. Billy Joe's two rapid shots echoed his and two of the Mexicans spun round on their heels before collapsing to the ground. The fourth man turned tail and ran back into the *cantina*, his pistol still undrawn. Buck's slug caught him between the shoulders as he was framed in the doorway, flinging him into the *cantina*, dying fast and loudly.

'There's another one of the bastards inside, Billy Joe!' Buck yelled. 'Down him before....' The sharp crack of a rifle from the front of the building blotted out the rest of his words.

Billy Joe grinned. 'Chulo's seen to him, Buck!'

Buck reloaded his pistol and sheathed it. As he took hold of his horse's reins he heard a slight noise behind him. He spun round, hand clutching for his pistol again and glimpsed a black object come hurtling out of the barn. With a sickening, bone-crushing thud the striking hammer hit one of the Mexicans Billy Joe had shot on the side of the head, knocking him off his knees and stretching him back on the ground once more. Killing him for sure this time.

Josh came out of the barn and picked up his hammer. 'The sonuvabitch was drawing a bead on you, Mr Taylor.' He smiled at Buck. 'It was as I said, it's a bad day when a *gringo* can't help another *gringo* in time of trouble.'

'Amen to that, Mr Josh,' replied Buck with feeling. He turned and looked at Billy Joe. 'And thanks to you, son. You got me out of as tricky a situation as I've ever landed myself in. When we get back to Texas I'll buy you a beer with the greatest of pleasure.'

Josh leery-eyed Buck. 'You ain't a gold seeker at all, are you. Mr Taylor?'

Buck smiled. 'No I ain't. Mr Josh. Meet Billy Joe an associate of mine. If you'd care to come round to the front of the *cantina* to see how my other pardner, an Apache kid, has fared I'll tell you why we're here. Unknowingly you've played a part in our game, Mr Josh.'

The owner of one of the horses tethered outside

the *cantina* lay on his back on the ground, left foot raised, trapped in a stirrup iron. A growing reddish-stain discoloured the front of his chest. There was no sign of Chulo.

'Things so far have gone our way Billy Joe,' Buck said. 'But we've got to work fast and clear up this mess before any more of the Don's men ride in. I don't want to stick more grief on to this village than it already has. Bring your horse and the burro in and water them. There's a trough at the back of Mr Josh's barn. I reckon Chulo will be making his own arrangements.' When Billy Joe had left, Buck turned to Josh. 'I'd be obliged a heap more if you could help a fellow *gringo* out again, Mr Josh, a Texas Ranger *gringo*, by giving me a hand to load the dead Mexicans on to their horses so me and the boys can dump them well away from the village.' He then briefly told the smith why the three of them were in Mexico. Josh listened with slack-jawed disbelief.

Josh shook his head. 'Mr Taylor,' he said after Buck had finished. 'You and your *compadres* are the craziest *hombres* I've ever had the pleasure to meet.'

Buck grinned. 'We've won two rounds against the Don already, Mr Josh. And when me and Billy Joe crossed the Rio Grande we didn't expect help from a full-blood Apache and an uppity Nigra slave. We've got to play our winning hand to the full.' Buck's face hardened. 'But that don't mean pushin' our luck by standin' out here all exposed. I ain't gone completely *loco* to think that the three of us can take on the whole of the Don's gang, so let's get these bodies loaded up and Chulo can lead us back into the mountains to give us the cover we need to work out where we're goin' to hit the Don next.'

A stone-faced Buck watched the five bodies turning slowly in the breeze at the end of the hanging ropes, strung on sparse-leafed branches of a small grab of timber on the edge of a trail Chulo had told him was used by the Don's *bandidos*. Chulo had wanted to lift the dead Mexicans' hair before Buck had them strung up. Buck persuaded him not to carry out the gruesome ritual with a sweetener of one of the dead men's nearly-new Winchester repeater and .44 Colt pistol. The rest of the weapons, less a few bandoleers of reloads, Buck gave to Josh, to keep for the day when, he hopefully told the big smith, he had the Don on the run, and the villagers would want to take part in the kill.

'It was you telling me that you'd strung up one of the sonsuvbitches that gave me the idea to do likewise, Billy Joe,' Buck said. 'Seeing his men swingin' by their necks the Don will know that it's *gringos'* work. He accepts that the Apache will pick off some of his boys from time to time, but Texicans doin' it, so close to his front porch, will disturb him more than somewhat, wonderin' who we are and how big a bunch we are. He's bound to

raise a big hunt to try and track us down; that
should drag in all his men, clear the way to the
border. His boys won't be so happy gettin' a taste
of the medicine they've been dishin' out. Could
cause some unrest amongst them. All to the good
if it keeps the bastards from ridin' north into
Texas.' He pulled his horse away from the trees.
'OK, Chulo, you lead us to the Don's hideout.'

Billy Joe noticed as they began to make height
that Buck had suddenly taken to wearing a big
knife like Chulo's on his hip. His blood chilled,
realizing that from now on in if they sneaked up
unawares on any of the bandits the killings would
have to be silent. This near to the Don's hideout
guns would be too dangerously noisy to use.
Silently also meant close-quarter killing, body to
body close. And he was only getting used to killing
at long range. But when that time came, Billy Joe
told himself, he wouldn't let his two *compadres*
down. At the next halt for a breather he would ask
Buck if he had a spare Bowie.

SEVEN

Buck and Billy Joe, keeping low down on the rim-line, looked into the depths of the broad, well-watered valley that was Don Jose Valiente's hideout. Behind them, further down the ridge, Chulo was guarding the animals. The whole valley was dotted like a township with huts of all sizes, shapes and construction. There were as many campfires as there were huts, round which they could see women busily preparing meals and men sitting around them or moving between them to talk to nearby *compadres*. The valley was as full of activity as a hornets' nest.

There were at least, as far as Buck could make out with his first sweep of the glasses, three stone-built buildings, one of them with a stoop built on to the front of it. Buck pointed towards it.

'I reckon that one a bit fancier than the other huts is our friend, the Don's place. Outside that stone building at the back of it I can see boxes of dynamite. That must be the Don's arsenal.'

The more he viewed the scene below him the

deeper depressed Buck became. He lowered his glasses and turned to Billy Joe.

'Billy Joe,' he said, sour-faced. 'My second plan ain't goin' to work either. I knew the Don could raise m'be forty or fifty assholes when he goes out raidin' but it seems that every lawbreaker in northern Mexico is walking about down there. If a company of Rangers rode in there they'd be cut down to the last man.'

'Does that mean we're going to pull out, Buck?' Billy Joe said.

'You and Chulo do what you feel you oughta do,' Buck said. 'But I'm a Texas Ranger, and under orders. I told the capt'n that all I was intent on doin' was to pinpoint the Don's hideout then I'd report back to him. Then he would lead the company across the Rio Grande, take the shit that would come flyin' his way for crossing into Mexico without clearance by his political chiefs. He was willin' to take all that grief if it meant the end of the Don. I'll have to go back and tell him that bringing the company here would get the boys massacred.'

'Your plan could still work, Buck,' Billy Joe insisted. 'Not the way you reckoned on, enabling the Rangers to get here safely and have an eyeball-to-eyeball battle with the Don and his boys. I'll admit that when I first rode out I was after seeing every sonuvabitch who rode with the Don dead. But that was a crazy hope. Now I'll settle for seeing the Don being cut down. We do as you suggested, harass him, not to draw his men from the border, but to get him to come out in the open.' Billy Joe favoured Buck with a determined, unwavering look. 'If I can get him in the sights of my Henry for three seconds, he's on his way to hell. By golly, from here I can piss down on the Don and that's the distance I ain't lengthening between me and him. I could climb down this ridge till I get within rifle range of his porch and plug him when he steps on to it if that didn't mean I'd be selfishly putting yours and Chulo's life at risk.'

'It will have to be something spectacular, like putting a real fire under the Don's ass,' Buck said, 'to get him mad enough to come out of his hole to personally hunt us down. Killin' a few more of his *muchachos* won't do the trick. He'll soon cotton on to the fact that there's only three of us doin' the hell-raisin' and leave it to his men to rope us in. And we can't hang about too long slipping through the net he'll throw over the territory.'

Billy Joe gave a mad-ass, 'Glory Boy' grin. 'It was a real fire I was thinking about starting, like blowing up the Don's armoury with those crates of dynamite you saw. Send a coupla sticks winging over on to his front porch to shake him up a mite more if I can get within throwing distance. I reckon the Don's hurt pride and not wanting to lose face in front of his men, will make him do what we want him to do. How does that grab you, Buck? You've had more experience in making plans than me.'

Buck thought over for a while what Billy Joe had

said. The kid's words made sense. Cut off the head
of the rattler and the snake would die. Die in so
much as it wouldn't come crawling across the Rio
Grande again. He gave an inner grin. What the
hell had he to lose by going along with Billy Joe's
plan? His life? He put that commodity on the line
every time he went out on a patrol. His chevrons
and pension? By heck, the capt'n would give him a
big medal if he came back with the news that the
blood scourge of the border was dead. He let the
grin show on his face.

'Back there in the village,' he said, 'Mr Josh
called me crazy. I don't know how he would tag
you, Billy Joe, if he'd heard what you've just
related to me. But being that I'm recognized as
being *loco* I'll fall in with your plan. And some old
fart has to be around to keep you two hellions in
check.' Face hardening he continued, 'Once this
shindig has started these mountains will be
swarming with men, full-bloods, breeds, *hombres*
who can sniff out sign as good as Chulo can. We
won't get much sleep or eatin' done and we'll have
to crap on the move like our animals then hide the
durn mess.'

'I know that, Buck,' Billy Joe said, jaw jutting
out at a stubborn angle. 'But that's the chance I'm
willing to take. I owe it to my pa and ma and kid
sisters.'

Buck didn't want to dampen Billy Joe's
enthusiasm by telling him that getting out of the
valley, once the ruckus started, wouldn't be as

easy as getting into a sleeping camp. Having no other plan of his own he said, 'We've been actin' foolhardy since we crossed the river, Billy Joe, and we're still alive. I see no pressing reason to change our lifestyle now.'

'It will have to be me and Chulo who goes into the valley,' Billy Joe said. 'No offence, Buck, but you ain't the fastest and most silent of climbers, your cursing could be heard all over that canyon. Once we're down there if we can grab a coupla hats and serapes we should have no trouble moving around. Most of the *muchachos* will be drunk or with their women.'

'I've aged something terrible since I took up ridin' with you, Billy Joe,' grumbled Buck, good-naturedly. 'I reckon we can't do anything more up here, let's get back and put the plan to Chulo. We'll have to rely on our red brother's natural sneaky skills to keep us alive over the next few days. Then we'll get ourselves some shut-eye in before the big event. A tired man stacks the odds against himself.'

Sergeant Isidro Amayo stood outside his hut smoking a cheroot, watching the revelry that was going on around the campfires. Soon it would quieten down once the liquor took hold or some of the men led their women away to pleasure them. Lying on his bed was a plump-thighed woman but duty overrides the delights of humping a willing and ready woman. A man never neglected to carry

out the Don's commands, unless he wasn't too
fussy about staying alive. The Don, Amayo
thought enviously, was enjoying his woman. A
hot-assed *señora* who lived in a grand *hacienda*
sixty miles away and whose husband was in
Mexico City on business, leaving Amayo in full
charge of the camp.

Tonight the camp was crowded with *comancheros* and *bandidos* from Sonora escaping the
bandido clearing-out sweep the *rurales* were
ranging across the State. For a price the Don was
giving them sanctuary. To Amayo the newcomers
were a pain in the ass. They were causing trouble
among the *muchachos* by lewdly eyeing their
women and he had no doubts that the dogs were
casting equally lusting gazes at the armoury and
the cases of new *gringo* Winchester repeating
rifles it held. If any of them were stolen the Don
would remove his balls and dangle them in front
of his eyes.

Amayo had a deeper problem chewing away at
his insides than just making sure that no trouble
broke out in camp. The shot dead men swinging
from the trees had been found. The reading of the
tracks around the hanging trees told of three men
being involved in the killings. The one riding the
unshod horse could only be an Apache. The other
two horses were *gringo* iron-shod. A *gringo* had
been responsible for the killing of the men
guarding the cattle. He had also left a *compadre*
hanging from a tree as some sort of deadly

message for the Don. Was he one of the *gringos* who had done the latest lynching? Could he be a Texas lawman, or an *hombre* with vengeance in his soul? And who was his *compadre?* And how did it come about that a *bronco* Apache rode with them? Amayo's head swam with all the unanswered questions he was putting to himself.

He had also been told that men sent out several days ago to drive off some Apache who were stealing the Don's cattle had not yet returned to the camp. Yesterday Amayo would have blamed their non-showing up on the Apache, caught and killed in an ambush. Not now. He knew as if he had read it in a book that if ever the missing *muchachos* were found, nearby would be the tracks of two *gringos* and one Apache horseman.

Amayo was a cold-blooded, unemotional killer but his inner feelings were beginning to stir uncontrollably. Not the normal fear of a man under fire but the dark fear of an unknown danger, his Indian blood accepting that the Spirits of Death come out of the after world to take a man through the Gateway of Death. He looked up at the rapidly darkening ridges above the valley. The same blood was telling him that the *gringos* and the Apache, shamans or humans, were there waiting to pay a death call on him and the Don. He shivered.

Amayo crossed himself, wishing the Don was here so that he could unburden some of his fear on to him. Then cursing his weakness he threw away

his cheroot and walked across to the nearest fire
to share some *muchacho*'s *tequila* to lay his fears.
Behind him a disappointed, frustrated girl drew a
blanket over her nakedness and, curling herself
into a ball, tried to go to sleep.

EIGHT

'If you have to use this pig-sticker, Billy Joe,' Buck said. 'Jab for the belly and cut upwards, or a quick ear-to-ear slash across the throat. Both are kinda messy but unless you're a real expert in handlin' a knife like Chulo here, it's the easiest way to kill a man for sure.'

Billy Joe looked with fascinated horror at the Bowie Buck had placed in his hand. He fought hard not to throw up on hearing Buck's matter-of-fact, stomach-churning advice, and the thought of the fearful agony the ten-inch blade would cause when plunged hilt deep into the soft, vulnerable flesh of a man's stomach.

Sensing Billy Joe's upsetting thoughts, Buck, narrow-eyeing him, said, fatherly, 'Are you sure you want to go through with it, kid? I'd be foolin' you if I told you that knifework was a pleasant business.'

'Yeah, yeah, I want to go through with it,' Billy Joe said, angry at showing his weakness. He drew his gaze away from the knife and slipped it into the top of his pants. 'I'll be OK, Buck, honest.' He was still far from feeling OK but his pride wouldn't prevent him from fully playing his part in bringing the Don to book, as Chulo was prepared to do.

Chulo, face war-painted up, had lost all his inhibitions about fighting alongside his enemies, the white eyes. He had only joined up with them because he was honour bound to do so. He owed them his life. But a born fighter has an affinity with men who are of his kind. Their skills with a gun, especially the younger white eye, proved that they were real warriors. Now the young white eye was prepared to fight like an Apache, hand to hand. Close enough to smell the fear of an enemy that short time between the knife thrust and him knowing that he was no longer for this world.

Chulo unslung a small leather bag hanging from around his neck and poured out some of the yellow-coloured powder it held into the palm of his left hand. With a dampened forefinger he stirred the powder into a thin paste. Reaching over he painted war marks on Billy Joe's face. He had also decided that when it was the time for the chief of the men who had killed his sister was destined to die he would let his brother warrior, who had a greater loss to avenge, have the honour of killing him.

Buck grinned at the surprised Billy Joe. 'You should have no bother with those bad-asses down there, Billy Joe. Just lookin' at the faces of both of you scares the shit outa me. But remember, boys,' he said, serious-voiced, 'if things get out of hand you both get back up here, *pronto*, savvy? I don't want to be left fendin' for myself in this wild country or I'll never make it back to El Paso.' He grinned at them. 'Then we'll have to try and come up with another plan.' He gave them one final look. A searching assaying look he had given his Rangers many a time before committing them to some action but could see no signs of weakness of their resolve in either of their faces, Billy Joe's as savage hard as Chulo's. He touched them both on the shoulders. 'Good luck, *amigos*. Remember, I want no dead heroes.'

Billy Joe cursed softly. They had come to a dead end. Their progress halted. Chulo, who was leading, had suddenly stopped and raised a warning hand. Billy Joe moved alongside him and tentatively stretched out a foot in the darkness below him. It swung in mid air. Their way down had ended above a sheer face of rock. In the daylight, when he and Chulo were searching for the best way down through Buck's army glasses, if they had spotted the bluff they could have possibly discovered a way round it. Now, in the dark, it would be a time-wasting exercise, the rock strata could run along the whole length of the valley wall.

Billy Joe could, however, calculate how big the drop to the valley floor was by the nearness of the

campfires and the loudness of the voices of the
men at the fires. Ten to fifteen feet he opined. Not
too high for loose-limbed youths like him and
Chulo to drop, if they knew that the ground
beneath them was free of leg-breaking rocks. And
they could do it silently so as not to alarm the two
men whose bulky, blanket-draped figures he could
see silhouetted against the dying embers of a
campfire.

Before Billy Joe could make up his mind to risk
jumping or move along the side of the ridge to try
and find a rock-free way down, he heard Chulo's
whispered, 'Stay,' and he saw Chulo lower himself
over the edge of the rock and drop out of his sight.
He drew out his pistol, ready to give what support
he could to Chulo, wondering how he could get
back up again if the alarm was raised. He cast a
quick glance at the other fires, also beginning to
die down, but many men were still moving around
the camp. If they both got down OK they would
have no trouble at all in strolling across to the
armoury without being challenged.

He looked back again at the nearest fire, he
could no longer see the two men sitting at it. Then
came a night bird's call from the darkness below
him, twice more it sounded. Chulo. Billy Joe
hesitated no longer. He sat down on the edge of
the rock, breathed a short prayer, and jumped. He
landed safely, but with a bone-jarring thud on soft
earth and thick long grass, Chulo's steadying
hands preventing him from falling on to his face.

Straightening up Billy Joe's hand brushed against a body and, looking down, he saw another dark bundle near it. Chulo's teeth gleamed white in the dark in a savage, scalp-taking victory grin as he handed him a broad-brimmed plains hat and a none-too-sweet-smelling *serape*. Chulo, he thought, had already drawn blood. He hoped when it was his turn in the game he would be as successful.

As Billy Joe had reasoned, the camp being too crowded for every man to know each other, the pair of them, walking boldly, casually stopping for a few minutes at some of the fires, got within yards of the armoury without being challenged. Then they hit a snag. A man with a rifle slung over his shoulder was sitting outside the door of the armoury. Billy Joe looked at Chulo, pointing with his chin at the sentry. 'You'll have to see to him, Chulo, and take his place. We've got to keep things as they seem.'

Chulo favoured him with an understanding nod and, with another one of his wolf-grins, ghost-like he slipped away from his side. Soon, Billy Joe impatiently told himself, he would be able to play his part. He wiped his sweat-sticky hands, raised by excitement, not fear, he believed, against the seat of his pants then drew out his pistol. Cocking it he held it down by his side, hidden by the *serape,* ready for instant use.

He watched the sentry get up from his chair and walk to the end of the building into the deeper

darkness away from the fires, as if to stretch his
legs. Then only a close observer of the scene as he
was would have noticed the brief blurring
movements of shadowy figures at the side of the
armoury, only he knowing that the sentry
walking back to his post was Chulo. At last the
time had come to light the fire under the Don's
ass, and he had to fight the urge not to dash across
to the armoury to get it started.

Billy Joe slow-walked the short distance to the
hut, keeping up the pretence of a man wandering
aimlessly around the camp. Once there he quickly
got down to the business at hand. A levered pistol
barrel soon sprung the rusty padlock and the door
of the armoury was open. Billy Joe cast a quick,
nervous glance over his shoulder; nothing unu-
sual seemed to be happening at any of the fires, no
questioning shouts. As he was carrying the boxes
of dynamite inside he did get some reaction. A
shout from someone at a fire between the armoury
and the Don's hut of, 'Hey *amigo*, don't go raisin'
too much sweat or you'll not have the strength to
pleasure your woman when you get her to bed!'
That advice was echoed by ribald hoots and
laughter by the rest of the men at the fire. Billy
Joe, taking a chance, stepped into the firelight
and raised his hand in an obscene gesture at the
'*amigos*', as any *hombre*, ill-tempered with having
to work when everyone else was enjoying
themselves would do.

'*Amigos*,' he muttered, 'when this bang goes off

some of you will be doing your next pleasuring in hell.'

By the time he had stacked all the boxes in the hut, tight up against long wooden crates that he took to be full of rifles, Billy Joe had raised more than a sweat. His nerves were almost stretched to a breaking point. What Chulo had for nerves puzzled him. He was sitting there seemingly unconcerned as though he was squatting on some lonesome ridge contemplating on whatever Apaches think about when they're on their own.

Billy Joe broke in half several sticks of dynamite, piling the powder in a heap on the ground, then placed some more sticks on the powder. Grabbing another handful he stuffed some of them in his shirt, the rest, breaking the caps off, he used as a long fuse, trailing the powder out of the hut, alongside the wall, and as far away from the hut as he could without attracting the unwelcome attention of the *bandidos*. And far enough away, he hoped, for him and Chulo not to be hit by the debris when the charge was fired.

He walked back to the armoury and looked across to what Buck thought was the Don's hut. He would have taken great delight in dropping two sticks of dynamite through one of the windows then the three of them could ride back to Texas, the job they came south to do completed, his and Chulo's honour satisfied, But there were too many men hanging about the place to get in

close enough to the hut to push the dynamite
through. Calculated risks could be taken, indeed
had already been taken ... acting just plain,
mad-assed stupid could only get him and Chulo
killed for damn all. Also the Don could have a
woman inside with him and Billy Joe balked at
hurting a woman. In a few minutes time the Don
was going to get shook out of his bed; a stick of
blasting powder going off on his porch might give
him the idea that he was the target of the raid.
That, thought Billy Joe, would really get the
son-of-a-bitch out into the open come daylight.

He struck a match on the heel of his boot and lit
the fuses of two sticks of dynamite, shielding
them with his body till the fuses had fizzed and
sparked halfway down their lengths. Only then
did Billy Joe turn and throw them at the Don's
hut. The first stick, sparking its way through the
night sky like a miniature comet, landed on the
corner of the Don's porch. The second fiery stick
dropped short, falling closer to the fire, from
where the men had mocked Billy, than to the hut.
They both exploded simultaneously. The two
thunderous flashes illuminated men flung every
which way like rag dolls by the force of the blast.
In the silence that followed Billy Joe heard the
screams of men in pain and confused shouts of
alarm.

To keep the panic growing Billy Joe yelled out,
'The *Federales* are shelling the camp, *amigos*!' to a
bunch of men running towards the sites of the

explosions. He heard their retreating footsteps in the dark as they sought safe havens from the non-existent threat. He bent low and put a match to the powder, watched the flame furiously licking its way to the armoury for several seconds, then said, 'OK Chulo, let's get out this valley. The old *gringo* will be worrying his heart out about us.'

To cover their withdrawal Billy Joe threw a stick of dynamite into a deserted campfire to the left of him, causing an instant explosion that sent them both staggering forward a few paces and showering them with red-hot embers. Then the earth trembled beneath their feet and sound waves bounced off the valley walls with the strength of a strong wind as the armoury blew up. The roof lifted then blew apart and a mushroom of red-tinged flame, along with the contents of the shed, shot skywards, illuminating the whole valley for an instant of time like a flash of storm sheet-lightning. The walls shattered, sending out pieces of masonry in a deadly hail that cut men down as efficiently as a volley of canister shells.

The encampment was in uproar. Riders, men up on wagons, on foot, headed in a shouting, cursing mass for the pass out of the valley. Billy Joe had seen more orderly cattle stampedes. He grinned at Chulo, then both of them had to fling themselves sideways to escape being trampled into the ground by a bunch of spooked horses.

A man rose off the ground in front of Billy Joe

and clutched at the lapels of his coat. 'What's happening, *muchacho*?' he asked in a drunk's slurring tone.

Billy Joe told him the same lie. 'It's *Federales*, they're attacking the camp with cannon, *amigo*.'

'*Federales*?' Amayo rocked unsteadily on his feet and took another pull at the bottle he was holding in his right hand. '*Federales* attacking Don Jose Valiente?' he said, face twisted in disbelief.

A second explosion sounded from the ruins of the armoury and a fresh gout of flame further lit up the valley and Amayo saw the warpaint marks on the *muchacho's* face he was questioning. '*Madre Dios*, the Apache!' he gasped and the *tequila* bottle fell from his hand as he made a grab for his pistol.

How the Mexican knew that an Apache was one of the men who were tracking down the Don's gang was of no immediate importance to Billy Joe, but his life was. His hand gripping the Bowie seemed to move on its own volition thrusting forward in Amayo's belly. He felt the sudden gush of blood running warm and sticky over his hands and wrist as he sliced upwards with the big blade.

Amayo's shrill dying scream as the knife cut deep into him froze Billy Joe's face into the fixed rictus grin of a skull. In the last agonizing seconds of his life Amayo saw that the Apache had the blue eyes of a *gringo*. A *gringo* Apache? Amayo died with another unanswered question locked forever in his brain.

Billy Joe, sickened from the smell of blood,

shuddered and pushed the dead Amayo away from him, the killing knife still lodged in his body. He didn't know if he would have the will to kill again if challenged and he almost ran to where they had descended into the valley. In spite of how Billy Joe felt Chulo thought that his brother was truly a warrior now. An Apache could not have killed so quickly and cleanly.

Buck had been thrown off his feet by the shock waves of the explosion. Fortunately for him he had fallen backwards and rolled part way down the reverse slope of the ridge and only suffered a few minor bruises, eased by a long and colourful spell of cursing, knowing that if he had fallen the other way he would have got down to the valley floor in record time without touching the sides. And sure as hell, he thought, in no fit state to have indulged in any cursing.

The last time he had seen an explosion of that size had been during the war when a blue-belly shell had hit an ammunition wagon and he began to worry about Billy Joe and Chulo not getting clear of the big bang, remembering the far distant casualties the exploding wagon had caused. Amayo's death shriek told that at least one of the boys was still alive. Hearing a man's painful death cry without the sound of a shot meant knife work, Chulo's expertise. Buck hoped that it was Chulo who had despatched the Mexican to hell. Knifing a man to death isn't something a Christian-raised boy like Billy Joe can easily sleep off. Buck heard a slight scrambling noise below him and dropping flat on the ground he looked over the edge, pistol pointing in the direction of the sound. He grinned as he picked out two dark shapes climbing towards him. He sheathed the pistol, got to his feet, and reached out a helping hand. 'Had a nice party, boys?' he said, conversationally. 'I heard the ruckus all the way up here.'

The explosion woke Josh up; still half-asleep he got out of bed and padded barefooted across to the window and looked out. He saw a red glow reflected off the clouds above a ridge of the mountains. Then he heard the second bang. Josh grinned. The Texicans were giving the Don some of his own medicine, and then some by the sound of things. M'be, he thought, it would put some backbone into the villagers when they got to know that the Don could be hit hard. Make them keen to resist the next time the *bandidos* came to take their women. They had extra guns now to help them to fight back.

NINE

Buck kept a constant watch on the encampment. Behind him Billy Joe and Chulo sat round a small, smokeless fire drinking coffee and eating warmed-up beans. Billy Joe, gaunt-faced, dead-eyed, sat unseeingly, spooning down his beans. No doubt, thought Buck, still picturing the man he had knifed. Chulo's face, Apache-like, didn't register his feelings, but Buck reckoned that beneath that gravestone mask he must be feeling cock-a-hoop. Both of them had done a hell of good job last night. The valley looked as though a whole regiment had fought a pitched battle across it.

The heap of rubble and fire-blackened timbers of what was the armoury was still smouldering. The windows of the Don's hut were blown out and only a few feet of porch clung lopsidedly upright. Upturned wagons lay dotted around the valley and men were gathering together a sizeable row of bodies. And the camp was a good deal emptier. Buck put that down to the fact that there must have been more men in the camp than just the

115

Don's regular band of cutthroats. Whoever they were it seemed like last night's mayhem had made them move out fast to seek a safer camp. So they were back to the three of them facing the Don's *muchachos* again, with another round definitely in their favour.

Only one thing soured Buck's insides: he couldn't see any sign of the Don, or anyone who was dishing out orders to the men clearing up the camp. He had never been within seeing distance of the Don but men who had, and were lucky to still be alive, had told him that he was a tall man, dressed in a Jim Dandy officer's uniform. Of course, the fancy-pants son-of-a-bitch could have been killed by the dynamite but he had seen no uniform-garbed body being carried out of the hut or could not pick out through his glasses a suchlike-dressed body lying around anywhere in the valley. The Don, he finally concluded, must be away on a business or pleasure trip some place. That wasn't a major setback to their plan in any way. The Don would still tear his hair out when he gazed on the damage and the killings the boys had sicced on him and would want his revenge by tracking down who was responsible for him losing face.

It would mean though that they would have to stay out in these mountains longer than he had reckoned on. It could, conceded Buck, as an old campaigner, present a problem eating-wise. They could, or at least Chulo could, trap silently any

eatable critter there was living this high up –
guns would be too dangerous to use – to eke out
their dry rations. Feed for the horses was another
matter; there wasn't much of what they could eat
growing on these bare ridges. It could mean Chulo
making a trip across open country back to San
Pedro for grain for them. All in all, Buck thought
soberly, a lot was riding on Chulo's natural skill:
his and Billy Joe's lives no less.

Buck walked down to the campfire. 'Boys,' he
said. 'You sure had one helluva ball down there. I
ain't seen the asshole whose benefit it was laid on
for so it looks as though we've got to stay in
Mexico longer than we thought. I'd be obliged if
you, Chulo, could find us a well-hidden base camp
where we can leave the horses. If we're pressed
hard we can haul-ass over these sawtooths on
foot, make less tracks for someone to sniff out
than we would sitting up on our horses. Though I
reckon they'll not be keen to get themselves
organized to set up a hunt for us till the Don gets
back, but we should keep an eye on them from this
ridge, then we can get advance warning of any
trouble brewing up for us. We'll take it in turns.'
Buck grinned at Chulo. 'Being that you Apache
can smell trouble further than we white eyes can
see it, you can take the night watch.'

Josh stepped outside his barn at the sound of a
screeching wheel and saw two wagons being
driven towards him, their piled-up loads covered

with tarp sheets. Beside the two Mexican wagon
drivers another six men were riding as escorts, all
of them North Americans. That gave Josh the
knowledge that the merchandise on the wagons
was valuable. Noticing the sharp-eyed looks he
was being subjected to from the pinched-assed
faces of the Americans he judged that the goods
were guns, ammunition and whiskey for the Don
and his men.

A regular, profitable trade for some enterpris-
ing man, rich enough to hire hard men to make
certain that the goods got to their buyer and not
stolen by the Apache who were always on the
lookout for easy pickings of guns and whiskey.
But it was the first time any gunrunner's wagon
had paid a visit to San Pedro. The screeching
wheel told him why.

'Well lookee here, fellas.' It was a tall
thin-shouldered man wearing a tattered, well-
stained duster who spoke. 'A big buck Mex coon.
Are you the smith in this dog-shit dump?'

Josh's hands, clasped behind his back, squeezed
tight till they hurt, imagining that they were
round the thin man's scrawny neck. He forced
himself to smile a big coon's inane, happy-go-
lucky grin. 'I sure am, boss. I reckon you want
that back wheel fixin'. I could hear it running hot
afore you cut off the main trail.'

Not wanting to seem too uppity in plantation-
slave custom he didn't bold-stare the thin man.
The mean-faced bastard would not hesitate to

shoot down a Negro who he thought was acting cocky. It was time, Josh thought, to eat crow. And by hell he'd had plenty of practice in doing that. It had been his life till he had crossed the Rio Grande. The Rio Grande wasn't the River Jordan, leading to the promised land, but once in Mexico he had been treated as an equal, not as a slave, by the Mexicans until the Don and his *bandidos* came into the territory. But he was faring no different to the rest of the villagers. The Don treated them like shit as well. Even so it was a good life here in San Pedro and a prideful foolish action could lose it for ever. He didn't think it foolish when he had backed up the play of Mr Taylor and his two boys. Then he wasn't on his own.

'You guessed right, Nigger.' The same man was doing the answering. 'And if you fix it up real good m'be I'll pay you.' He cold-grinned his *compadres*. 'Ain't that so, boys?'

Josh was suddenly reminded of when, as a young boy out collecting berries in the woods, he had stumbled into a clearing in time to witness the last few seconds of a Negro's life as he hung choking to death at the end of a rope slung over a branch of a tree. The looks on the white-men's faces as they watched the kicking and bucking of the Negro as he fought a futile battle for life-giving air were the same lynch-mob grins he was getting now. Just as suddenly Josh decided that the sons-of-bitches were going to die. His pride wouldn't let him be pushed back any

further. What he had to do was to win some time.
Time to contact Mr Taylor and ask for his help. By
the bangs he had heard last night it looked as
though the Don had lost some explosives and
guns. If he was to lose what was on the wagons it
would be further proof to the *pacificos* that the
Don could be beaten if they got up off their knees
and fought back. If he couldn't make contact with
Mr Taylor why, damnit, he'd bushwhack the
wagons on the trail himself to get even with the
thin-faced bastard.

'I'll fix it for you good, boss,' Joss said. He strode
over to the wagon and bent down and examined
the wheel more closely. He looked up at the thin
man. 'It only needs a new bearing and packing
with grease and it'll be OK. But the iron rim is
wearing thin in parts and you've got a rough
stretch of trail ahead of you, it could snap and the
wheel will spring. A broken-down wagon will
draw every Apache *bronco* roamin' the territory to
it like buzzards flocking to a dead mule. I could
put a new rim on for you but it would mean
staying here a few extra hours, overnight m'be, to
allow it to bed into the wood.' Josh waited,
outwardly calm and innocent-looking, inside all
screwed up with anxiety, for his lie to be accepted.

He saw the thin-man's face twist and scowl with
indecision. Wanting to be rid of the wagon's goods
as soon as possible so that he could get paid and
get back to where he came from to spend it,
against the chance that that haste might cost him

half his due, and his life. One of the other men made up his mind for him. Jerking a thumb in the direction of the *cantina* he said, 'There'll be someone in there softer and sweeter smelling than our horses to cuddle up to to keep us warm if we stay the night, Dave.'

'OK then, we stay,' Dave said. 'You greasers get this wagon unloaded *pronto*, so the Nigger can get to work on it, and see to the mules. Then load it back up once the wheel's fixed, ready for rollin' out just after chow in the morning. And keep an eye on the merchandise, savvy?' He switched his fish-eyed gaze back on to Josh. 'And make a good job of that wheel or me and the boys will be attendin' a lynchin' before we move out of this burg.'

With burning hate in his soul Josh forced himself to touch his brow in a servile gesture.

Josh, stripped to the waist, helped by Emillano, a youth who as a boy had been captured and raised by the Apache till he had managed to escape, worked till the sweat poured out of him, repairing the wheel and fitting a new rim in less than half the time it would have normally taken him. Josh stood back from the wagon, satisfied with his work, and the time he had gained for carrying out his plan to give the weasel-faced Dave and the white trash who rode with him, their just deserts. Before walking across to the *cantina* he told Emillano to saddle up two horses.

Remembering his position in the scheme of

things called life, that a Negro didn't go into a
saloon where so-called white men were drinking,
Josh just stood in the doorway waiting to catch
Dave's eye. Conchita, one of the *cantina* girls, was
sitting on Dave's knee, an arm wrapped round his
shoulders. On seeing him standing there Dave
ceased fondling Conchita's ample breasts and
waved for him to come in. He need not have
worried about Dave still buying his lie about the
wheel; none of them, with the amount of liquor
they had already downed, were in a fit state to sit
up on a horse and ride along a trail in the dark.
And knowing from personal experience how hot
Conchita's blood ran when aroused Dave wouldn't
have the strength to put his boots back on till a
longways after he intended to move out.

'The wheel's fixed, boss,' Josh said. 'Your
drivers are reloading the wagon. I'm ridin' out to
the next village, boss. I've a job to do there. If
that's OK with you.'

The big, unfettered breasts bouncing tantalizin-
gly close to his eyes, the thoughts of the delights
they offered, and the tequila he had drunk,
mellowed Dave's natural-born meanness more
than somewhat.

'You do what you have to do, Nigger,' he
mouthed drunkenly. 'I'll pay you your due in the
morning.' He leered at Conchita. 'Me and this
piece of sweet-ass are goin' to be kinda busy for
the rest of the night.'

Hoping that Conchita was extra energetic and

Dave would drop dead in bed in an effort to match her passion, Josh left the *cantina* and joined Emillano waiting with the two horses at his barn. His plan was working, so far.

Josh sat at the now dead fire, waiting, wondering whether or not his plan was going to keep running as smoothly as it had been, Or that it had all been based on too many chances and hopes; that his anger at wanting to put the gunrunners out of business, permanently, had made him think foolishly, harebrained enough to land him neck-deep in Shit Creek. So far he could see no signs of a response to Emillano's smoke-talk. Emillano had lit the fire, then laid green wood on the flames to make the smoke. By the use of a piece of blanket he broke the smoke column reaching into the sky into irregular patches. He repeated the message then Josh told him to put out the fire. Josh wasn't about to let everyone in the State of Chihuahua, *rurales*, Apache, *bandidos*, whoever, know of his presence.

He had seen no answering smoke but was hoping, again, that didn't mean that it not been spotted by the men it was sent for. He was banking on Mr Taylor and his fast-shooting boys keeping a sharp lookout from some high ridge. Chulo would know what the smoke message said, and be curious to want to see the Apache who was sending signals that he wanted to talk face to face with another Apache, *pronto*. Or so Josh was opining.

He was also aware that he was taking a big, and dangerous, chance that no Apache *broncos* would see the signal and come ass-kicking in on their ponies only to see a big stupid black man sitting on his butt to greet them. Before they had got over their surprise at seeing a Negro who was familiar with the meaning of Apache smoke talk and lift his hair, he would tell them where they could get their hands on two wagon loads of guns and whiskey. And, further more, he would be right obliged if they would let him join in the raid. Not for a share of what the wagons held but to satisfy his honour. Josh had been told that settling matters of honour ranked high in an Apache warrior's code. That's if the bare-assed sons-of-bitches savvied *gringo* talk he thought morosely. He could have kept Emillano with him to do any translating but he had sent him back home. It wasn't the boy's fight and he had suffered enough at the hands of the Apache. If anyone else showed up, why, he was just a dumb-assed Nigger whose horse had gone lame on him.

Chulo saw the smoke and thought that it was a signal between two bands of Apache. He reported his sighting to Buck and told him that if he went to the meeting place there was a chance, knowing that the Apache would have covered a great deal of the territory, they may have information of where the *bandido* chief could be. Buck gave Chulo the OK to make the trip. Fatherly he was also going to tell Chulo to look out for himself till he recalled that the Apache were the best looking-out-for-themselves *hombres* he had ever come across.

Josh was about to admit that his plan had been a failure. He could still see no sign of any rider's trail dust and in a few hours the light would have gone from the land. It looked as though the only option he had left to get even with Dave and his boys was to really try a one-man bushwhacking. Then with a suddenness that startled him, Chulo appeared out of the ground at his very feet. Grinning with relief, Josh stood up and shook his hand. Chulo had seen who it was sitting at the dead fire long before he had shown himself to Josh so none of the un-Apache surprise at seeing a black man and not a brother Apache was visible in his eyes when Josh gripped his hand.

'I've a letter here for the old *gringo*, Chulo,' Josh said. 'If he agrees with what it says I'd be obliged if you would let me know.' Josh grinned. 'The usual Apache way.'

Chulo grunted his assent and tucked the letter down the front of his shirt and, as silently and unseen as he had appeared, he was gone from Josh's sight. Josh sat down again and draped the smoke signalling blanket over his shoulders. Soon the waiting would be over. One way or another.

Buck, as puzzled as Chulo had been on hearing that it had been the blacksmith who had been sending the smoke-talk, read the pencilled scrawled words. A slow grin crept over his face as he finished his reading of the letter.

'Boys,' he said, 'Mr Josh writes here that by the bangs he heard last night he guessed that we had poked the Don in the eye with a sharp stick and asks if we're willin' to jab him in the other eye. Though we didn't actually do it to the Don I reckon that's a fair understanding of what you boys did last night. But, getting back to Mr Josh's letter, he says that there'll be two wagon-loads of guns for the Don comin' along the trail sometime in the morning. Just north of where he sent the signals the trail crosses a deep arroyo and somehow, he don't say how, he's goin' to arrange for one of the wagons to break down in there. Six men are ridin' shot-gun with the wagons. He's hopin' to join us and take part in the takin' of them if that's what we intend doin'.'

'Ain't that a bit risky, Buck, us going down on to the flat?' Billy Joe asked.

'If the wagons get through to the Don, Billy Joe,' replied Buck. 'All the good work you and Chulo did will have been for practically damn all. It ain't as risky as it seems comin' out of these hills. They're still hard at it burying their dead in the valley, don't seem inclined as yet to ride out and look for whoever caused them all that grief. If the Don gets back while we're away and he kicks-ass to get his *muchachos* mounted-up to start to hunt us down my bet is that these ridges will be the first places they'll scout out. Besides we can't let Mr Josh down, he's puttin' himself at some risk interferin' with the wagons and I owe him for saving my life. We'll see to the horses, Chulo, if you get the smoke-talk goin'.'

Against the red arc of the dying sun as it dropped behind the ridges and peaks of the Candelarias Josh saw an unbroken black thread of smoke. The Apache signal for yes. He gave a grim smile of satisfaction as he got to his feet and mounted up. Tomorrow was going to be a big day. He prayed it would go well for the four of them.

TEN

Josh had calculated right. After the wagon's rough passage across the stone-strewed bed of the *arroyo* the wheel he had tampered with came off as the wagon began to pull out of the wash. The back of the wagon dropped with a thudding jerk that threw its driver forward on to the ground beneath the iron-shod, panicky hooves of the two-mule team and tipped out most of its load. And effectively blocked the trail for the second wagon.

Dave swore a blue streak as he surveyed the splintered axle, the burst open crates of arms lying at the bottom of the *arroyo*. The driver, the blood from his caved-in head seeping into the dust was of no concern at all. Most of his curses were directed at Josh and he would have sent two of his boys back to San Pedro to nail the Negro's hide to his barn door if they hadn't stirred up trouble for themselves back there. It was trouble that six of them could handle; two men could find themselves in a hairy situation.

The trouble had started when that horn dog Cisco Platts had staggered out of the *cantina* and grabbed a young girl busy filling buckets at the well. The crazy-drunk son-of-a-bitch made to pleasure her right out in the open. The village priest, a little old greaser, tried to stop him. Cisco just hauled out his hogleg and pumped two slugs into him, killing him. The girl's screams and the shots brought the Mexs out their houses and if he hadn't pistol-whipped Cisco and dragged him off the girl, with the rest of the boys backing him up with their rifles, the Mexs would have cut them to pieces with their machetes and hayforks.

Instead of sampling the delights of a hot-assed *señorita*'s body he had had to sit up half the night making sure that his throat wasn't slit or his goods stolen. The damn wheel coming off had been the big Nigger's doing. He had seen him at the wheel and the bastard had told him that he was only packing some extra grease on the wheel bearing. Oh yes, black man, Dave said to himself, once I've got my due from the Don, me and the boys will call on you before we head for Texas and collect our due from you.

'Cisco,' he said, 'being that your hot pants got us into this shit you ride on to the Don's camp. Tell him how things are here. Ask him to send out some men and a string of mules to carry the crates from the busted wagon.'

'The only place you pilgrims are goin' is hell,' Buck shouted, standing on the lip of the wash, rifle held across his chest. 'You can make the one-way trip from here by goin' for your guns, or wait till I get you all to Texas and see you hanged for trading arms to the Don.'

Dave squinted up at the blurred figure with the blinding sun at his back. 'Who the hell are you, mister?' he snarled. 'Ain't no Yankee lawman got jurisdiction in Mexico.'

'My name is Sergeant Taylor, a Texas Ranger!' Buck called back. 'And my Rangers are all along this wash aimin' rifles at your black hearts. I don't hold with the niceties of the law when I'm dealin' with murderous scum like you.' Buck held up his rifle. 'This is my judge and jury. Your move, *amigo*.'

There was too much at stake, money, his neck, for Dave to back down even though it looked like he was pushed into a tight corner. Dave was a mean, murdering son-of-a-bitch but didn't lack the balls to make a fight out of it. He believed that a man isn't dead till he's stopped breathing. Dirty-mouthing all lawmen and their mothers and fathers he grabbed for his pistol.

Buck's two snap shots as he dropped to the ground hit Dave in the chest, flinging him backwards out of his saddle, his face twisting in a final spasm of pain. Billy Joe's shot brought another one of the gunrunners down. Chulo's shell only nicked the arm of one of the four men left before they leapt off their horses and sought shelter behind the second wagon alongside the driver who didn't want any part in the gun battle.

Buck was satisfied the way the small battle was
progressing. He had intended waiting till Josh
had showed up so that he could discuss with the
big Negro some joint plan of action, being that it
was his idea to start with. But, looking down on
the gunrunners together in a nice tight bunch, it
was too much of an edge to throw away. He still
had an advantage over them, bottled up behind
the wagon. Billy Joe and Chulo could work their
way along the bed of the *arroyo* and outflank
them. Force the bastards to break, retreat or
advance. Either way they would be a clear target.

Before he could signal to Billy Joe and Chulo to
start closing in on the gunrunners a ragged
sounding line of gunfire broke out along the
opposite rim of the *arroyo*, cutting into the
gunrunners before they had time to turn and take
on their new threat. Another fusillade flamed and
roared along the rim opposite him and the battle
was over sooner than he had expected. Warily
Buck raised himself and peered over the edge of
the *arroyo*. The gunrunners all looked dead, or as
near to it to have lost the will to fight. He stood up
and shouted across the gap, 'Mr Josh! It's OK for
you and your boys to come on out. There'll be no
more shooting from any of them down there!'

A wide-grinning Josh, flanked by eight of the
men of San Pedro stepped into view and began to
walk down the grade to the wagons, Buck and
Billy Joe doing likewise from their side. Chulo,
bred to always try and anticipate possible trouble,

stayed on watch on the rim of the *arroyo*. After all concerned, with handshakes and back-slapping, had congratulated each other for their part in the victory, Josh told Buck and Billy Joe of the anger in the village at the raping of a young girl and the shooting of a well-loved priest by the gunrunners.

'Though you gave them the idea of fighting back, Mr Taylor,' Josh said. 'Showed them that the Don could be hurt when you killed those five in the village. And they heard the commotion you raised at the Don's camp. The trouble those bastards caused, '– Josh pointed his rifle at the dead men, – only pushed them over the edge. With the extra guns you gave them they felt confident enough to do some bloodletting of their own.' Josh's face creased into a grin again. 'Especially when I told them that the two wild-assed *gringos* and their *bronco* Apache *compadre* were going to help them.'

As he finished speaking a whole stream of villagers came flooding down into the *arroyo*. While heaping praise on the riflemen at their success they began arming themselves with the rifles lying on the ground, those from the unbroken boxes and taking the dead men's weapons. Bodies festooned with bandoleers of shells they were ready for the next battle.

'Every man and boy in the village is here, Mr Taylor,' Josh said. 'And they're all for attacking the Don's camp and once and for all get rid of the bastards who've been grinding their faces in the dirt and using their women all these years.'

Buck looked at the eager grinning faces. 'They've got fire in their bellies that's for sure, Mr Josh,' he said. 'While I don't want to take anything away from what your boys just did it ain't the same as a real stand-up, lead-swapping gunfight. The Don's men, though they could still be shook up, will fight like cornered rats and the villagers could take losses. That could knock their enthusiasm for a fight on the head. We want some plan where the Don and his boys gets all the grief.'

'Such as?' Josh asked. 'They've worked themselves up for a fight. If they don't get one their blood will cool off and they'll go back to being dumb-assed *pacificos* again. Letting the Don ride all over them as before.'

Buck grinned. 'You're as bloodthirsty as Billy Joe and Chulo, Mr Josh. But I see your point so I've come up with an idea. I might tell you that it ain't the first plan I've made since we crossed the Rio Grande and they ain't worked out all accordin' to the way I originally figured but me and the boys are still here and a heap of the Don's men ain't. Before we discuss it I think that we should get all the gear the wagons carried back to the village in case the bad guys come snoopin' around. Use the mules and the horses, not the good wagon; leave that here.'

When the still jubilant peons had strapped the crates on to the animals and were ready to begin pulling out of the *arroyo* and back along the trail to San Pedro Buck explained his plan to Josh and Billy Joe.

'We draw the Don into our killin' ground, the village,' he began. 'Though he won't cotton on to the fact that's what it is. Along with frettin' just who the hell it was that wrecked his camp he'll be wondering why the arms wagons ain't showed up. He'll ride out and see the empty wagons and by reading the tracks know that they joined the main trail outside the village. Naturally he'll come into the village to find out why they rolled into San Pedro. When all unsuspecting-like he gets close enough we answer his questions before he asks them, with a hail of hot lead. Of course, Mr Josh, we'll have to get the villagers ready to repel the Don.'

'The Don being a suspicious-minded son-of-a-bitch,' Josh said, grave-faced, 'might have already made his mind up that the villagers had something to do with the stealing of his guns and come riding into San Pedro shooting.'

'It's up to me and my boys to make sure that he don't think along those lines, Mr Josh,' Buck replied. 'Chulo will ride along your back-trail wiping out all the tracks the mules and horses make. The only tracks the Don will see will be of three horses, two of them iron-shod. Sign he's already well acquainted with, believe me, *amigo*.'

'And we hang those dead gunrunners from the nearest trees, Mr Josh,' a stone-faced Billy Joe said. 'The same as we did with the five men we shot in the village. The same as I did with one of the first bunch of the Don's scum I met up with.

Like the hoof-prints the hanged men are our calling cards. You can bet on it, Mr Josh, that we've given the Don more to occupy his mind with to even consider the possibility that peons who he has terrorized for years have suddenly found the balls to fight back.'

Josh looked long and hard at Billy Joe and Buck. 'I thought you were hard *hombres* after I'd seen you in action outside my barn but you're harder and meaner than I reckoned.'

Buck thin-smiled. 'We ain't natural-born mean sonsuvbitches, Mr Josh. Why, young Billy Joe here, has a sweet young girl waitin' for him back in Texas. The Don wiping out all his family kinda turned him into a hard man. My sweet disposition has been soured somewhat by ridin' into situations where the Don and his boys have just paid a call. Those sights ain't something that nurtures the Christian love-thy-enemy line of thinkin'. Even Chulo has a personal score to settle with the Don. I reckon that your neighbours have just found some of that meanness.' Buck's smile warmed up. 'That's the end of the preachin', Mr Josh, it's time we were gone from here. As I said, I'll ask Chulo to clear up the trail behind you and I'd be obliged if you have the men who can handle guns armed up for when we get back to the village.'

Josh smiled back at Buck. 'Speakin' as a mean-minded Nigra, Mr Taylor, we'll all be ready when you and your boys ride in.'

ELEVEN

Don Jose Valiente sat at his desk, swept clear of
shards of glass and lumps of plaster, face growing
leaner and paler as he digested the disturbing
events that had befallen his command. Five of his
men shot dead then hung from trees, the
non-return of the men who had been sent out to
chase off the Apache cattle thieves and the
killings and dynamiting here in the camp. The
overdue arms shipment caused him concern. He
had a gut feeling that when he found the wagons
they would be empty and the men who were with
them, dead and hanging from some nearby trees.
He wouldn't need to look for tracks. He knew what
they would be, three riders, one riding an unshod
horse.

He wanted to shoot the men who had told him
all the bad news but he needed every man he had
to fight the trouble that was hitting him hard, and
unexpectedly. Amayo though, he would have
gladly shot dead. To be caught off guard by no
more than three men was a lapse of camp security

that warranted instant execution. He had met a deserved death. Through a jagged hole in one of the walls which had once been a window the Don could see the soot-blackened ruins of the armoury and a long straggling row of heaps of fresh dug earth. He shuddered. Was a pit going to be dug for him? He wasn't a superstitious man, didn't believe, like Amayo's part Indian of him had, in shamans, devils from hell, yet he was feeling the icy fingers of unknown fear clutching at his throat.

Just who were the men who rode iron-shod horses? The unshod horse rider, an Apache he thought, wasn't worrying him too much. Apache and Mexicans were natural enemies. The unknown *gringos*, and the ease with which they were able to kill his men, penetrate his camp with devastating consequences, were making him jittery-eyed. Seeing danger all around him. And the hanging of dead men was something that he, an expert in the act of inflicting pain, degradation and death, had never even thought of doing. He knew, from the hanging of the cattle guard, that it was a grisly message from the *gringos*. If caught he would suffer the same fate, to be hung from a tree like some common *gringo* cattle thief. Him, once a captain in the Emperor's Lancers, he indignantly thought.

The Don thumped angrily on the table top with a clenched fist. He was allowing himself to be as scared as the ignorant scum outside. Who the *gringos* were and why they were pursuing a vendetta against him didn't matter. What mattered was that they had to be tracked down before they struck again. However skilful the Apache was in hiding his and his *compadres'* trail they would leave some sign of their passage across the territory, his men would have to look harder. The Don got up from his chair, tugged down his jacket, centred his belt buckle and with his left hand gripping the hilt of his sabre, strode outside to organize the big hunt. While he had been dallying with the plump-assed *señora* things had got out of hand. Now the terror of the *gringo* border regions was back in command once more.

His first task was to find out why the arms wagons were late in reaching the camp. The *gringo* gunrunners, eager to get their money, were always on time. They could have had wagon trouble on the trail, he thought, without much conviction, resolved to accept his worst fears being realized, the guns taken. He didn't give a damn about the fate of the gunrunners. But it would be another damaging blow by the *gringos* against his pride and authority.

Buck gave his three captains their final orders. Chulo would range free outside the village where he would do the most good by acting as an early warner. Billy Joe would command the riflemen in the *cantina* whose rear wall, facing Josh's barn, had been loopholed for rifle fire. Josh was in

charge of the men in his hayloft, the gaping and
splayed planking offering a good flanking fire on
riders coming between the *cantina* and the barn,
the chosen killing ground. Buck had a squad, now
busy digging a curved trench behind a line of
brush. One point of the curve facing the *cantina*,
the other on the barn. Another line of fire in the
killing ground. If the Don and his men rode in the
way Buck was banking on.

'Remember boys,' Buck said to Billy Joe and
Josh, 'we'll only get one chance; a few minutes,
that's all, when the sonsuvbitches are bunched up
between the *cantina* and your barn, Josh. But no
one's got to fire until Billy Joe cuts loose. Then
they're to fire as fast as they can work their
cockin' levers, at the horses as well. Get them on
foot so that they can be picked off before they can
scatter. Break 'em here. Those still up on their
mounts will head towards my boys to get the hell
out of it.' Buck gave an all-toothed mirthless grin.
'If the *hombres* keep their heads low and aim fair
they should complete the massacre.'

A worried Don sat on his horse on the edge of the
arroyo waiting for the scouts he had sent out to
report back to him on any sign they had picked up.
The tracks at the empty wagons were, as he had
forebodingly surmised, those of the two *gringos*
and the Apache. Away to his left was a small
stand of alamos; he definitely knew who would be
swinging in the breeze in there so he didn't waste

his time riding across. And when his two men
returned they brought him no surprising news.
They had tracked the two iron-shod horses and
the Apache to the wood and saw eight men, six of
them *gringos*, all gunshot dead, hanging on the
end of ropes. Though they had scouted the wood
thoroughly they couldn't see any tracks of the two
gringos and the Apache leading away from the
hanging-trees.

The Don didn't believe that his scouts had
really put their noses to the ground. Seeing the
dead men had probably scared the shits out of
them. He didn't show his displeasure at their lack
of success in cutting sign, or his disappointment.
It didn't do to let his men know that the two
gringos' activities had also unnerved him.

'We'll follow the back-trail of the wagons,
muchachos,' he said, putting on a bold, confident
face. 'Somewhere along it the *gringos* must have
started to track the wagons and m'be got careless
and left sign pointing towards where they have
their camp.'

Six miles ride from the *arroyo* and still the only
tracks that could be seen were those of the mule
teams and the ruts of the wagon wheels. Then the
scouts shouted back to the Don that the wagons
had cut on to the main trail from the direction of
San Pedro. The Don smiled, and though it did not
reach his hard black eyes it was his first smile
since he had left the warmth and passion of the
señora's bed. There was just the possibility that

some man who traded between villages had seen
three riders trailing the wagons. Or the gunrunners themselves could have told the Negro
blacksmith while he was mending the wagon, the
only reason for the *gringos* driving into San Pedro,
that they were being trailed, and, like he was
about to do, ask the smith if any Yankee strangers
had been seen in or near the village. The Don
cursed. The Yankee pigs had to be somewhere;
they just couldn't make a few tracks then vanish
into thin air. He jerked his right hand out and the
tropa swung right to raise the dust along the San
Pedro trail.

Chulo had been trailing the Don since, at the head
of his men, he had ridden out of his camp.
Watched him at the *arroyo* as he waited for his
scouts to report back. Scouts; Chulo gave a
disparaging sniff. If he had been on a lone killing
raid, not part of the old *gringo*'s larger killing
plan, he could have arrow-shot them both. Lifted
their hair and taken their horses and weapons
without any danger to himself. Chulo's Indian
stoic mask loosened as his lips parted the width of
a knife slash in a smile of bloodthirsty pleasure
when the Don led his men along the trail to the
Mexican village. The old *gringo* thought with the
cunning of an Apache. Truly there would be a
great killing.

Buck sat on the adobe parapet wall of the village

well, the waiting chewing away at his guts. It had
been two days since the taking of the guns and
everything was ready, as prepared as a military
untrained peon force could be in two days, to give
the Don a bloody nose. He had told the villagers to
go about their normal business, unless that meant
leaving the village, but when they heard the
church bell ring out to run like hell to their
allotted posts, not forgetting to take their rifles
and shell belts.

The problem now was to keep the peons'
new-found fighting spirit blowing hot. Even
trained troops start losing their aggressive edge if
the start of a coming battle is constantly delayed.
Another day or so of waiting for the Don to make
his move, Buck thought, and his hastily mustered
soldier peons would cool off and revert back to
their time-honoured existence as bowed-head
pacificos. Buck saw the sun's reflecting rays
flashing from Chulo's signalling glass. The Don
was on his way. The thinking and worrying were
over. It was about to happen for real. It was the
peons and their grit who would decide the
outcome, one way or another, victory or defeat. He
grabbed hold of his rifle and stood up, yelling, 'The
sonsuvbitches are comin', Billy Joe!'

Billy Joe, sitting on top of the church bell-tower,
yanked at the bell rope several times before
running downstairs to take command of his men.
Buck watched with an old campaigner's experi-
enced eye the peons running, without any show of

panic, to their designated posts, the stable, the *cantina* and his trench, calling out to each other their good lucks. The women and the children hurried to the masonry-built church, well away from the battleground, for better protection. Buck gave a satisfied grunt. If they held under fire the Don and his boys would never ride out of San Pedro.

The Don noticed that the village was as quiet and deserted looking as it always was when the peons saw the dust of his *muchachos* approaching their village. The Don smiled in grim understanding. That was the way it should always be. The spineless *pacificos* knowing that he, Don Jose Valiente, held their lives, and their women's honour, in his hands. Though there would be no time this visit to allow his men to indulge in that right. Their lusts of the flesh, women and tequila, came second to hunting down the two *gringos* and their Apache *compadre*. The man who m'be could point the direction the hunt should take he could hear working in his barn. To the disappointment of the pleasure-seeking men the Don led them to the rear of the *cantina* and drew them to a halt by a sharp raising skywards of his right fist outside the blacksmith's barn. A fierce all-round scowl indicated that they hadn't to dismount.

Buck swallwed hard to ease the tightness of fear in his throat. The dust haze the bandits' coming had caused had cleared enough for him to see what looked like a whole brigade of horsemen. To further relieve his alarm he told himself that the real count could only be thirty to thirty-five men. He gave the peons next to him in the trench a pinched-assed grin. 'Don't worry, *amigos*,' he said, voice lyingly confident. 'There'll be plenty of the sonsuvbitches left for us to down after your *compadres* have done their bit.' Then silently, but fervently, he willed Billy Joe to set the war going before any of the bandits dismounted and spread themselves around the village seeking women and liquor and he and the peons would lose all their edge, and their lives.

Billy Joe was well aware of Buck's urgent desire for him to cut loose but this was the first time he had seen the Don, and within easy shooting distance, so the chance of putting a Henry shell into the Jim Dandy-uniformed son-of-a-bitch was too big a temptation not to take. The delay in opening fire was that the Don kept weaving and bobbing on the far edge of the press of riders, at times obscured altogether from his vision along the barrel of the Henry. Reluctantly, not wanting his personal feelings to jeopardize the success of Buck's plan, he picked a lesser target and squeezed the trigger, blowing a killing-dead hole between the shoulder-blades of a man close to the Don, and starting the carnage.

To the Don and his men the single shot was the herald of all hell breaking loose as the *cantina* and the upper floor of the barn erupted flame and smoke. Men and horses were cut down amid yells and squeals of pain, killed or wounded twice over by the non-stop, short-ranged barrage of rifle shots. Men thrown out of their saddles by rearing horses if not already dead or wounded risked death or injury under the wildly kicking hooves of wounded, pain-mad horses.

The Don felt a hammer blow on his left shoulder. His hands lost their grip on the reins as, groaning with pain, he collapsed across his horse's neck. A riderless horse bumped into his mount causing it to stumble and throw him to the ground, landing heavily on his wounded shoulder. The extra pain almost made him pass out. Eyes blinded by tears of pure agony he struggled to his feet, crouched low to protect himself from the mêlée of kicking and stamping horses. A horse and rider brushed past him and the Don made a grab at a stirruped boot. Hysterical, he cried, 'Pull me up!'

But it was every-*hombre*-for-himself time and instead of a helping hand from one of his subservient *muchachos* the Don got a vicious slash across the face by a heavily wielded quirt. His anger at such treatment by one of his men made the Don insensible to his fresh pain and fresh blood streaming down his cheeks. He let go of the boot and drew out his pistol and put two shots into the rider's face as he was about to bring down the quirt for a second strike. The man vanished over the other side of his horse.

The Don dropped his pistol and grabbed hold of the reins, pulling savagely at them to stop the frightened animal rearing and bucking while he, unsteadily, raised a foot to put it into the stirrup-iron. Fear of being shot down like a dog or trampled to death gave him back the strength his wounds were draining from him to pull himself up onto the saddle. Keeping flat on the horse with bullets still whistling ominously close to him the Don quickly decided, loss of face or not, it was quitting time. Only death faced him here. He saw a bunch of his men making a break for it, firing their pistols left and right as they spurred their mounts out of the village the opposite way they had ridden in. Digging his heels into his own horse's ribs he followed in their dust.

He almost screamed out his fears as gun flashes suddenly flared along the brush stretching across their line of escape. Whoever the *gringos* were, Texas lawmen, bounty hunters, they were expert in military tactics. It was like charging the *gringo* line at Bueno Vista again. Men and horses began to fall in front of him and not having the strength to turn his mount around he pressed himself lower along the horse's back and let it have its head. A few strides on and it gave a heart-stopping stumble then, miraculously, regaining its feet, rose in the air and the Don saw the riflemen in the trench and one of the *gringos*, in the split-second of time it took the horse to clear the trench. A quick look over his shoulder as he

raced away from the village showed that he had
been blessed with another miracle. He seemed to
have been the only one to have broken through
the ring of gunfire alive.

Straightening up in his saddle he began to
breathe more easily, and think of living again. His
first priority was to get his wounds attended to.
The amorous *señora* would see to that. Then
somehow he would have to try and get back to the
camp; he had gold and silver bullion buried there.
Not enough wealth to support another band of
muchachos till they earned their keep by their
raiding but sufficient to keep him in comfort in
Mexico City till he sorted out a new future for
himself.

The Don's right-now-time took a sudden turn
for the worst. He heard his horse give out a harsh
choking cough and its front legs folded up beneath
it, throwing him over its head. This time his fall
did knock him unconscious. Chulo slowly lowered
his rifle. He could have killed the Mexican chief
but that would be the young *gringo*'s honour. He
knee'd his horse into a slow trot towards the
huddled heaps of the Don and his dead horse.

For several minutes Billy Joe hadn't observed
any answering gun flashes from the Don's men so
he yelled for his men to cease firing, to let the
gunsmoke disperse to see if there were any of
them capable of continuing the fight. Not for any
belated Christian charity for them: the killing and
raping of Texans had forfeited their right to be

offered a soldier's choice of honourable surrender. This battle had been waged under the rules the Missouri brush boys had fought under during the war, the black flag, kill-or-be-killed boys, the Don's own rules. Only up till now he had been doing all the killing. But Billy Joe reckoned that the horses deserved a better deal. He told his men to stay on the alert then, warily, he stepped outside, pistol drawn, ready to throw down on any *bandido* playing dead hoping to get a shot at him. He hoped that if that happened his excitable riflemen could control their itchy trigger-fingers or he would end up plugged full of his *compadres'* shells.

Josh, likewise alone, came out of the barn and for a moment or two they surveyed the killing ground. Seeing the twitching and writhing of badly wounded men and horses, hearing their cries and groans. Stone-visaged, Josh said, 'This slaughter-house will need cleaning up, Billy Joe. The horses at least want putting out of their misery.' Raising his voice he shouted, 'OK *amigos*, you can come on out! The fight's over!'

Cheering and waving their rifles above their heads in victory salutes the peons poured out of the barn and *cantina* to congratulate each other, soon to be joined by their *compadres* from the trench noisily expressing their part in the winning of the battle. Those of the peons who had been wounded, mainly those in the barn, slightly injured by flying wood splinters, proudly displayed their red badges of courage to their *compadres*.

'We did it, Buck,' Billy Joe said soberly, still looking at the dead and wounded men and horses as the old Ranger came up to them. 'Though I can't see no sign of the Don among them, unless the sonuvabitch is trapped under one of the horses.'

'The bastard got away,' Buck replied. 'But it wasn't without collecting a shell or two in his evil hide. As his horse jumped the trench I could see blood all over his face and it looked like he'd got a busted left arm.'

'Damnit!' Billy Joe spat. 'I want him dead not just winged, that's why I came to Mexico. I'll saddle up and pick up his trail, if he's wounded it'll slow him down.'

Buck grinned. 'The Don won't have got as far as he reckoned on, Billy Joe, not with Chulo out there watching the back door. I heard him fire off one shot a while back so I opine that the Don's escape attempt has come to a sudden and permanent halt. Chulo, being an Apache gent, will want his two *compadres* to be there at the Don's end. You go, Billy Joe. Getting the Don was only what I'm paid to do, it's personal business for you. I'll stay with Josh and see to the wounded before the women come out of the church and start cutting them up with machetes and suchlike tools.'

Slowly, arm and face on fire with pain, the Don came to, and saw his dead horse. He blessed his saints for saving his life a third time though now he would never make it to the *señora*'s hacienda, not on foot. He would lie up close by, tend his wounds the best he could then, come night, he would sneak back into the village and steal a horse. In spite of the seriousness of his situation the Don's nostrils flared in arrogant anger. A bunch of unwashed, ragged-assed peons weren't going to grind him down to their level.

Gingerly he got on to his feet and wiped the caked blood and dust from his eyes and saw the Apache, sitting on his horse, unmoving as though carved from wood. The Don's nerves twanged as though he had been shot again. It hadn't been a wild-aimed shot from the village that had killed his horse after all. Sobbing, the Don turned and, half-walking, half-running he stumbled along in a blind panicky bid to escape his known fate. An impassive-faced Chulo let him go a few paces then, unslinging his bow, he notched an arrow and shot it into the fleshy part of the Don's left leg. Billy Joe heard his high-pitched girlish scream and rode in the direction of the sound.

Billy Joe drew up his mount alongside Chulo. As dispassionately as the young Apache he looked down at Don Jose Valiente, his bloody, pain-contorted face, his animal-like moaning as he clutched at the shaft of the arrow sticking out of his thigh. His tunic and fancy lace-frilled shirt a sticky mess of blood and dirt.

'You sure don't look like a Don now, *señor*,' he said. 'But I reckon it's the way you deserve to look for all the killing and suffering you and the scum

you ran have been responsible for. I came to
Mexico to kill you or see you hanged for what you
did to my pa and ma and two sisters on your last
raid into Texas. But you lying there like a mangy
cur dog ain't worth wasting a shell on. You're
going to die, the villagers of San Pedro will see to
that. They'll be coming out looking for you soon
and they'll take great delight in stringing you up.
It'll make their day, first wiping out your boys
then the big chief himself.' Billy Joe pulled his
horse round. 'Let's go Chulo, he won't be
wandering far, not with one of your feathered
sticks in him.'

The Don began to cry, his tears for what he was
losing, the power, the wealth and all the pleasures
it had bought him. And he heaped curses on the
two *gringos* and the *bronco* Apache who had
toppled him from his throne, destroyed his life.
With the superhuman strength of the madman he
now was he regained his feet and drawing out his
sabre aimed a wild slashing cut at Billy Joe's legs.
Billy Joe, sensing danger, twisted ass in his
saddle, pistol swinging round with him. Chulo,
being what he was, had never relaxed his guard
and was quicker in his reaction to the Don's
unexpected attack. Another arrow hissed on its
deadly way piercing the Don right through his
neck.

The Don staggered back, coughing blood, his
sabre falling unblooded to the ground. Billy Joe
held the Walker on him till he sank to his knees

and fell forward on to his face in the dirt. He heard the sharp brittle crack of the arrow shaft's snapping. A sound he would remember for a long time to come, the sound of the Don dying. His revenge paid in full. Only then did he sheathe his pistol.

He sagged back in his saddle and grinned sheepishly at Chulo. 'I know I shouldn't have turned my back on the sonuvabitch but we white eyes ain't as suspicious minded as you Apache. I reckon you've paid your debt you thought you owed to me and Buck, more than paid. I suppose now you want to ride back and join up with your people. I sure do. I've done all the killing I want to do, ever. And that's the truth, Chulo.'

'It has been a good killing time, Billy Joe,' Chulo said. 'You and the old *gringo* fight good, like Apache. You take the Mexican chief's hair, it is your right.' Chulo brought his horse round so hard that it almost sat on its haunches then took off in a four-legged kicking run that raised the dust high above Billy Joe's head.

'You take care, do you hear, Chulo?' Billy Joe shouted. An Apache warcry came bubbling back on the wind. He looked down at the Don. 'I suppose I'll have to haul you back to the village for some sort of a burial,' he said to the body. 'But you can keep your hair on. I ain't as bloodthirsty as my *amigo*.'

Billy Joe rode, shut-mouthed, head still throbbing and woozy with the *tequila* he had drunk. No more than three glasses, but for a youth who had never

tasted strong drink before the village-distilled
liquor had a throat-grabbing potency that would
have tested the drinking capacity of a real
elbow-bending man. No wonder the preacher
called it the demon drink, Billy Joe thought. How
the hell Buck could sit straight-backed in his
saddle, all smug-faced, after the amount of
firewater he had downed had him beat.

Then the old goat had led a willing, plump,
bouncy-breasted *señorita* from the fire to have his
pleasure with her. Billy Joe risked moving his
facial muscles in a painful grimace of a
remembering smile. He had done likewise. A
younger, slimmer girl had started kissing him,
putting her hands on him where a female had
never touched him before, hotting up his blood
much more than the tequila was doing. And again
as he had heard the preacher say on the Devil's
works, setting him lusting after the flesh of
women, and he couldn't do anything, or want to, to
suppress his burning urges.

'Don't fight against it,' Buck had grinningly told
him. 'You've killed your man, now you enjoy a
woman then you can call yourself a real *hombre*. I
reckon by the way you're getting all flustered it's
your first time.'

To his embarrassment the girl must have
known some English because she began to giggle
and her hands were all over him again.

He had brought the Don's body back to the
village slung across his horse intending, after

brief farewells and as soon as he had rations and water for the trip, to ride out for Texas and Mollie. That was till Josh told him and Buck about the *baile* the villagers were having to celebrate their victory over the Don, the two hard-assed *gringos* were to be the guests of honour. He had tried to back out of it but Buck had persuaded him otherwise.

'I can understand your eagerness to get back to Texas, Billy Joe,' Buck said. 'I hadn't reckoned on hangin' about this side of the border more than I had to. Capt'n Sinclair will be thinkin' that I've deserted, or got myself dead but as Josh says, they're puttin' on this shindig for our benefit and it would be right churlish of us not to accept their kindness in wantin' to give us a good sendoff.'

And the peons had. A full day and a half the night's worth of dancing, drinking and singing. He had tasted hard liquor for the first time. The delights of taking his first woman, as disappointingly quick it had been. Though to be truthful the *señorita* had had him. And the biggest, hellish headache in the whole of the state of Chihuahua and a mouth as dry as a salt pan. Not forgetting belated thoughts that somehow he had betrayed Mollie Bishop's trust in him.

As they neared the Rio Grande the sudden crack of a single rifle shot cut short Billy Joe's ruminating, cleared the *tequila* fumes from his brain and sent his and Buck's hands reaching for booted long guns. Then their alarm passed as quickly as it had been raised when, on a ridge away to their left, they saw the faint silhouette of a lone horseman. Buck took out his rifle and pulled off an answering shot skywards. In a blink of an eye, as though their sighting had been a trick of their nervous imagination, the rider had gone from the ridge.

'Why the young sonuvabitch has been ridin' shotgun over us till we reached the border, Billy Joe,' Buck said. 'Just in case some of his wild brethren jumped us. I sure hope he still thinks of me as his *compadre* if I run into him out on patrol in Texas.'

Once across the river they said their goodbyes and gave their handshakes.

'It's been a privilege and an honour ridin' with you, Mr Foy,' Buck said. 'A heap crazy but a privilege. And I'd be more *loco* if I asked you to become a Ranger when you've got a fine-lookin' girl waitin' for you.'

Billy Joe smiled. 'A man's entitled to go crazy at least once in his life. My crazy spell's worked its way out of my system so I've no hankerin' to be a Texas Ranger, and all the shooting that comes with the badge. As I told Chulo, I've done all the killing I want to do. But if you ever have to call men out to meet some big trouble you can call on me and I'll wear a Ranger badge. You know where you can find me.'

'I'll remember that, *compadre*,' Buck said. 'It could just so happen. We ain't tamed all the wild boys in Texas yet. Now you get ass-kickin' it to the Bishop place in case that daughter of his gets tired of waitin' for you and finds herself another beau.'

Mollie, doing her first chore of the day, saw the dust of a rider coming along the trail. She didn't have to wait till he had ridden nearer for her to know who it was. Not for one moment since Billy Joe had ridden off with Sergeant Taylor had she doubted his promise that he was coming back to pay court to her. The big doubts she had, caused her sleepless nights, was that Billy Joe wouldn't be able to make it back. He could have got himself badly wounded or dead in some Godforsaken place below the Rio Grande.

Mollie's good feelings waned slightly as she gazed down at her hog-swill splashed pants and shoes. 'Billy Joe,' she said out loud. 'You're ridin' in again when I'm feeding the hogs.'

Seth Bishop, sitting having his pipe on the front stoop, had also seen the rider coming up to the farm. He also noticed his daughter come rushing out of the hogpen, running towards the house. Grinning, he took his pipe out of his mouth and shouted through the open doorway, 'Ma! Get your best china out. It could be by the way Mollie's taken off our future son-in-law is payin' us a visit!'